Response From Early Readers

My Math Consultants and Beta Readers Chime In

A brilliant read ... cinematic.

Young readers will have a blast with this book ...

Skillful ... there is a special youthful ambition about the whole thing.

I'm certain this was the first time I've seen Bayes' Rule used in fiction, let alone in a captivating way! A very enjoyable narrative.

"Sasha with the Red Hair" felt like three stories wrapped into one ...
There is great value in the multilayered texture. Both the codebreaking and astronomics content are approachable.

The MLK story ... an excellent story with a crucially important message for young people in modern Western society. **The mathematics is simple but elegant.**

This was the first time I've seen Bayes' rule used in fiction, let alone in a captivating way! A very enjoyable narrative.

Both the codebreaking and astronomics content are approachable, not too technically heavy. I especially enjoyed the ending ...

Refreshing .... there is a special youthful ambition about the whole thing.

In this modern age as we face so many challenges, it is more important than ever that we embrace science and technology. Anything that encourages girls to take up STEM subjects is to be lauded.

(Her Secret War, Past Imperfect, The Bowes Inheritance)Stories, mystery and math go well together. "The Adventures of Ruby Pi and the Geometry Girls" is a welcome addition to literature encouraging girls with an affinity for math and a nudge for those who hesitate to take another look.

Math is not only about formulas and graphs. It's about its applications and illustrations. Tom has delivered 10 stories which ingeniously weave math into adventure stories. This intriguing book breaks the glass ceiling which prevents our young female students from pursuing STEM studies.

We must get girls to enjoy mathematics and to be artists in that field.

We need brilliant minds, women and men, of different social classes, ethnicities and schools of thought ...

We must teach mathematics from different points of view and different perspectives, as Tom has done in this collection of stories.

— Sandra Uve,
Author "SuperMujeres, SuperInventoras," from her Foreword

Must -read stories for readers of all ages who want to understand the value and some of the magic of mathematics. Tom's writing will keep you engaged. To especially those young readers who ask why we study STEM, get ready for a most surprising read.

I was not expecting the cipher!!

Teaching is my passion, and story- and game-based education are very near to my heart. Your storytelling is good. The footnotes at the end of the story are very helpful. It is a nice addition.

— Aditya Soni,
Game developer and Educator

In this outstanding collection, Tom addresses the chronic problem of our young women dropping out of STEM studies. His stories lend adventure to scientific thinking. These will no doubt stir an interest among readers and encourage them to find the solutions to their daily life problems by using Mathematics.

Tom's stories are challenging, ambitious, and **an excellent resource for developing problem-solving skills.**

"Sasha with the Red Hair" is thoughtful and surprising, like all Tom' s stories. **Exceptional ... a family drama disguised as an adventure.**

— Tanzeela Siddique,
Math Teacher

Tom, I love your project and I want to be part of it!

I love reading math problems with rich and interesting stories behind them, and this is definitely the extreme version of it!

History, drama and math make for an exciting adventure ... Tom communicates a love for math.

— Tommaso Pettinari,
Physicist, Code developer

"Ruby Pi and the Mystery of the Old Carthusian" is a tale of a young mathematician who uncovers the truths of the past, layer by layer, using probability and mathematical encoding. She leads the way in uncovering corruption.

It is an unusual adventure which takes surprising turns. I was pleased to find the irony. **I have never read anything quite like it.**

As a teacher, I believe it is vital to keep our girls engaged with STEM. **We need more of my students to become civil engineers like Rupa.**

– Pakeeza Sharafat,
Teacher

THE ADVENTURES OF
RUBY PI
AND THE
MATH GIRLS

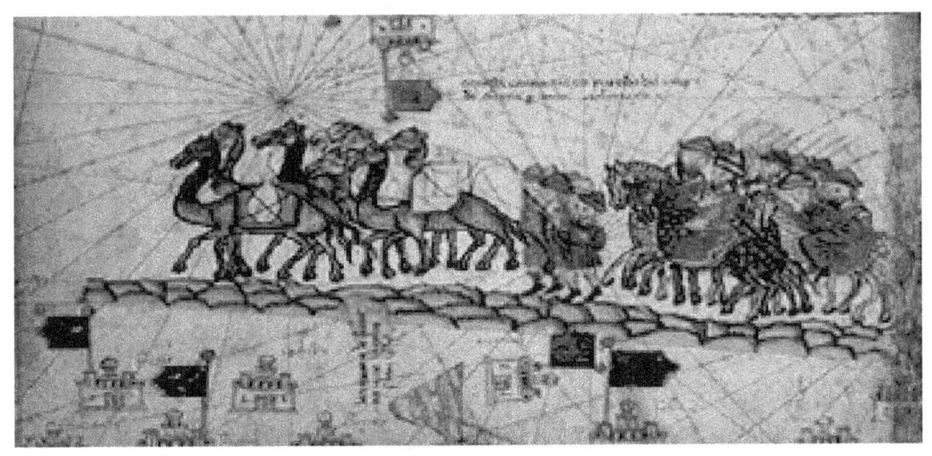

FIVE ADVENTURES

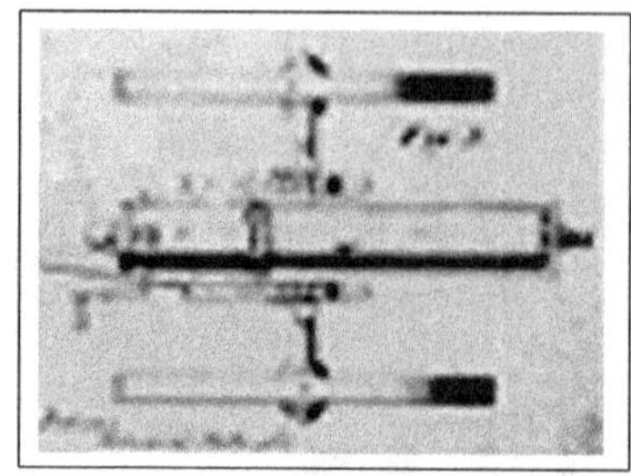

Contents

Rupa looks into the mysterious death of one of England's (and India's) foremost mathematicians. Her investigation arouses powerful forces. Ruby finds Bayes Rule to be a most useful tool as she combats personal danger and international intrigue.

Rupa plays Sherlock Holmes

Disgusted by her odd-ball family — her gambler mother in particular – Casey sets out to change their fortunes. The young card-counter depends on her mastery of rates of change to defeat the bandits who threaten them, one Mogollon evening.

Gambling and earth's curvature

Penelope West's school exercise turns into a bold prediction for September 16, 1992. Will a reclusive economist help her defy the markets and save her town?

Predicting Black Wednesday

Village life and castes are turned upside-down when Nalini makes a new set of calculations to save Third Aunt's life.

Volumes of a kiln

Uly takes the train to Moscow to collect an award for her work in Derivations, but as usual, her beautiful, red-headed sister Sasha steals all of the attention. When the family arrives to stay with a professor cousin, Uly becomes entranced with the Maya tablet the professor (Yuri Knosorov) is studying. The ensuing code-breaking triggers unexpected events.

A spoiled sister and an ancient Code

Afterword
Tom's Other Works

Credits
Cover by Iva Dukic.
Illustrations pages 6, 66, 71, 86, 102 copyright @2022 by Mai Nguyen
Silk Road illustration page3, swan page 79: Wikimedia Commons.
Geometric pattern, diagrams pages 60, 70, 92, 97,119:Wikimedia Commons.

ISBN: 978-952520-16-7 (paperback)
           978-952520-20-4 (ebook)

Empire Studies Press

Foreword
Sandra Uve

ODAY'S SCIENCE IS ARTISTIC, EXPANSIVE AND TRANSVERSAL. When we talk about scientific dissemination with a gender perspective, it is important to point out that intersectionality, with its systems of oppression in the face of coexisting identities, does not make any sense either in critical thinking or in the scientific method. We need brilliant minds, women and men, of different social classes, ethnicities and schools of thought, so that the world can continue to evolve. One of the best discoveries of this century, the detection of gravitational waves, was attributed to not just a single person but to many. Science knows no genres, only brilliant ideas that change our lives.

Not only are we clear about that, but science is currently being taught from a broader perspective, showing unlimited capacity. The amalgam of scientific branches, or what we know now under the acronym of STEAM, is a concept that especially motivates girls and teenagers, since it represents a much more flexible possibility when it comes to training, learning and specialization. Almost all the scientists and inventors in my book, however old, were multidisciplinary: from Ada Lovelace to Radia Perlman, who mixed algorithms with music and poetry respectively, to Concha García Monje and Mara Dierssen, who mix robotics and

We need brilliant minds, women and men, of different social classes, ethnicities and schools of thought ...

neuroscience with cinema and rock n' roll. The possibility of explaining to a girl the story of Mae Jemison and asking her not to stop dancing ballet because it will serve her to be an astronaut, has exponentially enriched my capacity as a science communicator. After years of challenging girls to look at science in a much more generous and creative way, I have been able to see the change in those who are now almost university students: the scientists of the future work from creativity, with all the freedom they have and valuing new stances with regards to possible gender exclusions.

However, of all scientific branches, mathematics is the one which needs the most dissemination with a gender and socio-emotional perspective. Mathematics generates anguish in children from approximately 5 or 6 years old. If you add to that from the age of 7 girls have already discarded mathematics because they are difficult, and socially they have been taught that the most complicated is intended for boys, we have a double challenge when it comes to disseminating and promoting this scientific branch. We must get them to enjoy mathematics and to be artists in that field. We must vindicate the pioneers who are still unknown and do not appear in schoolbooks. We must teach mathematics from different points of view and different perspectives, as Tom has done in this collection of stories, because this is when good creativity is generated and when the brain acts using all its superpowers: observation, curiosity, calculation, analysis, logic, empathy...

But above all we must give them current references in mathematics and put in context the social and future importance they have. Since I started my research for the project "SuperWomen, SuperInventors, SuperScientists" in 2015, life has changed a lot and therefore the needs are different. The world is controlled by experts in mathematics, especially algorithms. There is a very high labor demand that seeks

We must get girls to enjoy mathematics and to be artists in that field.

mathematicians and we do not have them yet. Jobs are waiting, so we must go the extra mile in disseminating mathematics. And we must do it from childhood and all the way through higher education. By standardizing mathematics in the classroom, we will ensure equitable and egalitarian training, so that as much talent as possible, without gender bias, enriches our science and technology system.

Sandra Uve
Illustrator, Writer and Scientist Communicator, Author
"SuperMujeres, SuperInventoras. Ideas brillantes que transformaron nuestra vida" Planeta, 2018
www.sandrauve.com

https://www.instagram.com/sandra_uve_official_account/

Author's Welcome

I am an English teacher and history buff. I have no aptitude for math. This makes me the perfect person to write these stories.

In these ten stories, I have tried to come at mathematics from different angles – colorful applications, how concepts and relationships were 'discovered' in historical contexts, placing the calculations in a variety of adventure scenarios.

The phrase "Geometry Girls" comes from the sixth story, "The Architect," when Queen Nala uses it sarcastically (and she pays for that!). It is meant to suggest all areas of applied mathematics.

I intend these stories to be challenging. I use words like 'susseration' and 'solipsistic' in the hope that my readers will look them up. Math is hard, and so is understanding the real significance of the Battle of Montcornet, or architecture in Africa.

I am offering links between you and applied math on my web site, www.themathgirls.com. More free material in this vein is to come.

Second and third collections of stories are also on the way.

A friend of mine used to work in Human Resources at a top tech company. Many, many candidates moved through the office, all badly wanting to work there.

The first meetings often ended with the interviewer saying this:

"I just have one last question before you go:

How many piano tuners are there in Manhattan?

Piano tuners, Manhattan – how many, would you say?"

The tech representative, of course, is not looking for a number but for a process. They want to see how you think.

Here is how your answer might go:

I'm not sure, but it certainly involves a few basic questions and answers.

How many people live in Manhattan? How many households? How many music schools? Music studios and plays on Broadway? How long does it take a piano tuner to tune a single piano? How long does a piano stay in tune?

On and on, in this vein, and you're hired.

One thing I think is that Mathematics is about problem solving. I think it is about using careful logic to crack all the codes that surround us, both in the man-made world and the natural world.

One thing I know is that you really, really need to understand both the mechanics of calculation and mathematical thinking in general as a lens to look at the world.

Your pal,

Tom D.
Seattle, WA

The Adventures of
RUBY PI

1. Ruby and the Mystery of the Shy Mathematician

SYNOPSIS: Rupa is called into action when a world-renowned mathematician, Anaan Warinda, is found poisoned. She and enigmatic Inspector Summerscale travel to Cambridge University. Rupa hopes to break the numerical and linguistic codes which protect Anaan's work. Shadowy foreign powers who also seek the notebooks descend. Rupa finds that Anaan was contributing to deadly new weapons systems. In the story's climax, Rupa is ambushed on a foggy night, on a London wharf ...

Bayes' Rule plays its part.

Prologue:
A Foreshadowing In Tirah

We had not accomplished more than a mile,
when about a hundred enormous vultures joined us,
and henceforth they accompanied the 21st Lancers,
flying or waddling lazily from bush to bush,
and always looking back at the horsemen.

— WINSTON CHURCHILL,
JOURNALIST, FROM HIS ACCOUNT OF THE BATTLE OF OMDURMAN (1898)

"See it, Seth!" said Dargai, aged fourteen, proudly. "Is it not handsome? Is it not warriorly?"

He waved his left forearm to and fro, so that the colorful beaded bracelet on his wrist could be shown to its best advantage. His young cousin had made it, to bring Dargai luck in battle.

"Are we not mighty?"

"Aye," agreed his friend Seth, aged fifteen." Who can stand against us?"

Their steeds snickered and pawed impatiently.

A sprawling force had gathered in the morning mist, in the foothills along the frontier. Tirah Valley lay in the northern district of Khyber.

The Raj — England's rule in India – was about to be tested.

In the Autumn of 1897, the many lands of Jambudweepa were the colonies of Britain.

History takes strange turns. A tiny isle off of Europe's coast had come to govern — in all things, large and small — the many and sprawling peoples and cities and territories of the vast Indian subcontinent, halfway around the world, in Asia. Queen Victoria's portrait was visible on stamps and in banks and penny-shop windows from Allapuzha to Srinigar.

The wonders of gigantic double-deck steel truss bridges over the canyons of Khyber and steam-powered locomotives criss-crossing the Punjab, measured against the racist laws, the casual cruelties, the taxes (paid in the Queen's currency), the sneering disrespect for all castes, all languages of the Ancient Lands — such were the paradoxes of the British rule in India.

Lately, new seven-year indenture contracts and rumors of Hindustani girls being trafficked on the wharfs of London had inflamed the tribes of the North. Resentment at the British Commonwealth's choke-hold over the regions of Aryavarta seethed and boiled over.

Orakzia tribemen had stormed the garrison at Pathan just a week prior.

Rebellion was in the northern air.

And now, early this fine morning, just south of the Kabul River, a host of warriors gathered on the slopes of Samana in the province of Kasmir. The Yorkshire 2nd, Fourth Gurkhas, Queen's Surrey and other British regiments waited at the base of the slope.

First blood would be drawn.

A British scout rode up to see the enemy host. He reigned in his horse and scampered back down the slope.

"Sarvada shaktishali!" came the rolling war cry.

The line broke and charged beneath waving banners.

"Jai bhagwan!"

Dargai held his sword high. Light sparkled in the colored beads of his bracelet.

The Battle of Tirah had begun.

1. The Call To Adventure

*I was hungry for stars, gulping light between
my jaws like an overzealous planet.*

— PRIYA KRISHNAN

*If you're not thinking like a Bayesian,
perhaps you should be.*

— JOHN ALLEN PAULOS

The story of Rupa's involvement in the case of the deadly Charterhouse tontine became well-known in Carthusian circles. Word of mouth a brought a variety of new clients coming to the door of her firm, Childress and Associates, Engineers.

Rupa had never been so busy.

So it was no surprise that she was late to the Pyradhakrishnan family dinner table that Thursday evening, as night was falling.

They all held off starting, only nibbling at the tomatoes scattered generously across the salad lettuce, until the favored daughter of Little Mumbai arrived.

"Rupa!" called the younger sister, Narinder, as the door opened. "Sit by me. Curry and raisins!"

Mother and Miss Deepa and Father watched Rupa rush in and remove her shawl and set down her books.

"See how Rupa dresses!" said Deepa to her own daughter, Surat, Rupa's cousin.

"Professional. Nothing to attract attention."

"The *angrejon* covet the Oriental woman," echoed Pryanka the Elder, nodding her head to add special emphasis. It was a sentiment she expressed often. Uncle Banjeet clucked in agreement.

"The English abduct our Indian girls," stated the old woman. "Down by the wharfs ..."

Rupa was seated.

"I'm starved!" said Eshaan, Surat's active younger brother.

"Grace," answered Father.

They reached out, each family member, to hold hands with the person next to them. Eshaan slapped Surat's hand away before she grabbed it and held tight.

"*Aham vaishvanaro Bhutva praninam Dehamashritaha,*" said Father, drawing out the syllables of the traditional grace in order to torture Eshaan, who was now acting out the seven stations of hunger.

"*Pranapana Samayuktah Pachamyannam Chaturvidham.*"

"Next year in Madras," added Pryanka.

"Don't say that!" corrected Mother. "London is our home. Our lives are here now."

"Please get the cat down from the table, Eshaan — " said Surat.

Plates were passed around. Steam rose as covers came off, releasing rich aromas. Serving spoons and ladles of gravy went into action.

"Jaiden was arrested again," said Deepa.

"What?" replied Father. "Does he think he'll make a flowery speech in Trafalgar and the next day 24 million Kalkatans will go on strike?"

"Serve your husband first," said Banjeet to Mother. "He's taking Ojasvat's shift."

"Why, Dad?" asked Narinder.

"Ojasvat is sick, and we need the extra money," replied Father. "Rupa takes the QCE in September — "

"I told you! My firm pays half!" protested Rupa. "Don't you ever listen — "

"This family doesn't take handouts," stated Father gruffly.

Just then, the doorbell rang.

Eshaan bounced off his seat to see who it was.

"Pass the rice, please," requested Narinder. "The yellow rice — "

"Who can that be?" asked Mother. None of the neighbors ever bothered to ring.

"Why would they strike in Kalkata?" asked Surat.

"Strike what?" asked Narinder. "What would they strike?"

"Rupa!" called Eshaan from the front door.

"A policeman! For you."

Deepa and Mother exchanged glances. Father and Uncle Banjeet rose, dropping their napkins on their chairs, and went to the door.

The diners remained seated at the dinner table, craning their necks to see who it was.

They heard Father murmur.

The door swung open and then closed shut.

Their friend and neighbor, Mahit, chief of the neighborhood watch, entered, hat in hand.

Beside him stepped a fresh-faced London Metropolitan Inspector. He wore a long tweed coat and heeled leather shoes, as a banker or lawyer might wear. A badge hung at his neck

"Hello," the visitor said with a nod.

"I am Special Investigator Daniel Summerscale.

"I do beg your pardon. Calling at such an hour.

"I wondered if I might have a word with Miss Rupa."

The young Inspector showed his badge to Mother, to Deepa, then to the ever-suspicious Pryanka.

Rupa came around the dining table and introduced herself.

Inspector Summerscale spoke loudly enough for all to hear.

"Anaan Warinda is dead."

"No!" cried Deepa.

Gasps came from all around the dining room. Hands on mouths at this most unexpected news

Anaan Warinda, the eccentric Tamil mathematician, was a well-known figure among the *pravaasee* (as the Indian ex-patriates of London were sometimes known). His scholarly successes were a point of national pride. His career at Cambridge and his publications were closely followed.

"We would very much like to borrow you, Miss," continued the Inspector, looking at Rupa, "for the investigation."

"Of course," she replied. "Give me a moment to change."

"Vardan is not here," said Rupa's Mother, following her into the bedrooms.

"Does it have to be right now?" Uncle Banjeet asked the Inspector.

"I'm afraid so. It looks like murder."

"But it's night-time!" cried Narinder.

"I'll go with her," said Father.

"You can't. The *Mirabelle* docks at eight," Banjeet reminded him

"Can Mahit accompany her?" Miss Deepa asked the Inspector. "Everywhere. At every step."

Both the Inspector and Mahit himself assured her that this would indeed the case.

Father fetched Mahit a folding billy-stick from the mud room, beyond the kitchen. He looped the handle over Mahit's shoulder.

"But why do you need me?" asked Rupa, who had reappeared, with jacket.

Deepa handed Rupa a roll of *naan* flatbread wrapped around curried chicken, the *naan* itself wrapped again in a cloth napkin.

"I know nothing of police work!"

Mother embraced Rupa as she made for the door.

"The *mathematics*, Miss," replied the Inspector.

"It's the mathematics."

Mother whispered for her daughter to take extra care this night.

On The Train To Cambridge

In 1720, an Indian youth of 16 was taken from Madras,
shipped to London by Captain Dawes, and gifted to
Mrs. Elizabeth Turner, who christened him 'Julian'.
Mrs. Turner forced him to dance and croon ... before guests.

— ARUP K. CHATTERJEE

The train to Cambridge passes northward from Croyden station along the Great Eastern line, through the wooded districts of Watford and Luton and Stevenage. It is a rich and fabled landscape, where Henry and Edward once kept their royal forests.

"Both your face," said Rupa to the Special Inspector, "and your name, are familiar to me."

"Yes, Miss. I am Daniel Summerscale. My father's brother is David Summerscale, who teaches at the Charterhouse School. You met him during your recent adventure.

"It was he who recommended that I include you in our investigation."

"How did Anaan die?" Rupa asked Summerscale.

"Poisoned. He was found by one of the maids. In his rooms. No sign of struggle."

"There was no smell of almonds, so we've ruled out cyanide. We are inventorying the Chemistry Department, Hospital. Landscapers. The Coroner should have a preliminary report for us soon."

"Why now?" asked Rupa rhetorically. "Why poison him now?"

The train car leaned slightly as the tracks curved northward, and east.

"Who and why," continued the Inspector. "We believe his notebooks will contain clues ... "

"But the damn things are written in Sanskrit or some such. We can't make heads or tails of them.

"We're hoping you can, Miss."

"I am Hindu. Anaan Warinda is Tamil. But I will do what I can," said Rupa.

Outside, the greened hunting grounds shimmered under the starlight as the train made its way over the tracks.

"Did an angry student kill him?" asked Mahit. "Was there a love triangle, or some such? An issue of castes, I wonder."

Rupa looked at Summerscale. He knew more than he was letting on.

"We have our theories," replied the young Special Inspector evenly. "The local police have theirs. Conflicting theories. Nothing proven.

"Best I say no more until we're on-site. We don't want to bias your findings."

This explanation, while certainly true-sounding, left a great deal unsaid.

Rupa nodded thoughtfully.

"Ah. Here is the food cart. Would either of you care for a sandwich?"

"No. Thank you."

"Tea?"

Rupa shook her head.

Noting the deference with which the cart attendant and the conductor approached young Inspector Summerscale, Rupa looked around at the empty seats.

"Do we have this entire car to ourselves?"

"Yes," replied Inspector Summerscale.

"Did you ever meet Professor Warinda?" asked the Inspector.

"Yes," Rupa nodded. "Many years ago. We were on the same ship, making the crossing. I was six. Then once again, at a lecture he gave in Croydon."

"What was he like?"

"Very shy. Childlike. He loved cats."

The train seemed in good cheer, its speed and confidence increasing as the locomotive pulled them smartly through a landscape of gentle gradients and easy swoops.

"Those lights," the Inspector pointed through the window, on the train car's left or western side. "There. Can you see? That's the edge of Wessex Downs."

The food cart came and went again.

"So," said Summerscale to Rupa. "You're a snob."

Rupa looked at him.

"A food snob." He took another bite of his own sandwich (bologna).

"Let me guess. You find British food bland. Bland and lacking in both imagination and texture."

"Only a little," replied Rupa.

"It's not her fault,' explained Mahit. "Rupa's Mother is the best cook in all of West London."

"*Bayes Rule*," said Rupa as the train approached Luton.

"Ah," nodded the young Inspector.

But Rupa said nothing more.

"Who or what is Bayes," asked the Inspector, "and what might his rule be?"

"Thomas Bayes," answered Rupa, "was a minister. In the late eighteenth century. From Tunbridge Wells.

"He came up with a rule. It sounds simple.

"The probability of arriving at a true theorem improves upon the processing of new data.

"One can successfully revise a theorem as one acquires a fuller knowledge of conditions. In so doing, you improve the odds that you will solve it."

"I see," said Summerscale .

"Yet you are denying me this," concluded Rupa. "You tell me nothing."

"Well. I can tell you this much.

"We know that Warinda's sponsor, Professor Stagg, left the University on sabbatical in April. Since that time, we understand that Mr. Warinda has been more or less on his own. Unprotected, so to speak.

"Three parties in particular seem to have consumed him. Almost to the point of hounding, according to his colleagues at the Mathematical Society.

"First, a mathematical feud."

"The Dane — " said Rupa.

"Yes, the Danish ... enmity. It seems to have spilled over into a highly personal quarrel. Deep feelings on both sides.

"Second, a foreign power has been identified. Their agents have been trying to get Warinda's help on new weapons systems.

"Third, a domestic cabal. Internal to the Commonwealth. This group urgently sought his support. His ideas. His mathematics.

"We suspect that one of these three entities may well have poisoned the man. These are our leading suspects. Until we have more data, as your friend Bayes suggests."

The Inspector fell silent.

"Do you know what this feud was about?" Daniel asked Rupa..

"Yes. Anaan and a Danish mathematician named Lars Matthiesen," began Rupa, "had a disagreement. Over vectors, I think. The disagreement became a controversy when a Mathematics journal lost Anaan's rebuttal paper. Matthiesen was the journal editor. Then the controversy ... it grew. It grew over months and years into a bitter feud between the two camps. Yelling at conferences. I know that Matthiesen lost his tenure.

"Anaan had left the whole thing behind, I think," she concluded.

The train whistle sounded. It was a long, sad sound, warning cows and all living things in the vicinity away from a wheeled, fast-moving steel vector, a speed and a force, that would not be stopping.

"We may find out soon enough," remarked Daniel as he leaned back in his seat.

"If God wills it, none can thwart it," observed Mahit.

Rupa twirled the chain of her necklace.

The ruby at her breast, on the end of the chain, turned, catching glints of light, like a prism.

Outside the train windows, the fenced meadows of Luton looked on, emerald-dark against the backdrop of the constellations, silent in the topaz and sapphire cloaks of night.

Mystery Of The Notebooks // Trinity College

Don't look for it, Taylor.
You might not like what you find.

— PIERRE BOULE

Trinity College is one of the oldest, richest and most prominent colleges within Cambridge University. Isaac Newton attended Trinity College …

Walking through the grounds was a stroll through architectural history, so varied were the structures. Paved pathways cross-crossed the lawns. Students and faculty and those unfortunate in-betweeners, graduate students, were out, enjoying the summer night. They crossed through an open-walled corridor and came to Whewell Court, home of Anaan Warinda.

Several members of the College's Mathematical Society hovered around Stairwell 7 of the cloister, carrying lanterns, in an impromptu vigil for the late mathematician.

Blue-coated constables guarded the roped-off entrance. More uniformed men made room as the trio from London climbed the steps up to Warinda's third-story rooms.

The parlor was dominated by two very large Oriental rugs, a note-filled chalkboard and two large, framed pieces dominated the living room. One, a map of India and the second a print of *The Gross Clinic*, by the American painter, Thomas Eakins. A small plaque reminded all that it was a gift from the Belgian Mathematical Society. A narrow, cramped kitchen lay beyond the parlor.

"Here you are," said Daniel Summerscale as they entered Warinda's study.

They saw a comfortable – bordering on shabby – study crammed with blackboards, wall postings, sofas and warm colors. Bookshelves sagged under the weight of tomes. Two large Oriental rugs covered the floors, giving the place a homey feeling. Small square paper notes dominated by numbers in equations had been thumb-tacked directly to the thick, striped wallpaper.

A sweater was draped over the desk chair. A small side-room housed a neatly-made bed.

Piles of note-pads and foolscap — the distinctive lined, watermarked schoolboy paper, slightly narrower and slightly longer sheets than most – covered the desk and table surfaces. Stacked neatly across the surface of two desks shoved together stood a row of tan leather-backed notebooks.

Constables brought in an extra lamp and three small swiveling devices that pushed air.

"What's this?" asked Mahit, delighted.

"Electric fans," replied Inspector Summerscale. "American invention."

Mahit leaned his face close, so the breeze ruffled his hair.

The young Inspector rolled up his sleeves as he shifted a second fan to face in Rupa's direction.

In doing so, he revealed a long and ragged scar on one of his own forearms.

"Where did you get that?" asked Rupa.

"Nothing. Schoolboy squabble."

"No, it isn't," said Rupa. "You got that in a fight."

"*Ksatrivah,*" said Mahit, using the term for India's warrior-elite caste, who bear arms in times of war and govern in times of peace.

Rupa removed her jacket. She sat at Warinda's desk. She ran her hands along the flat surface.

She rummaged through the desk drawers until she found a magnifying glass.

She opened the first notebook. Here is what was written on the first page:

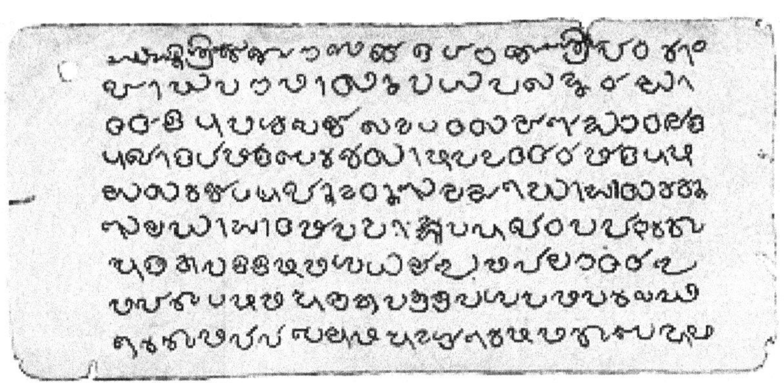

"Ah" said Rupa. "It seems we have our work cut out."

Neither Mahit nor Special Inspector Summerscale cared to interrupt Rupa, as she scanned through the pages, deep in thought. Now and then she would slow, granting long minutes of attention on some single detail. Now and then she switched from eyeglasses to the magnifying glass. She seemed to devise her own system of notations on one of the foolscap pads.

"I find myself devising explanations for all her movements and mannerisms," Daniel told Mahit, on the transom below, where they could enjoy the fresher air. "Tamil-reading mathematicians of Rupa's caliber did not grow on trees."

As time crawled on, Daniel became mesmerized. He gazed at the planes of Rupa's face, the texture of her skin, the forelock of hair that fell over one of her eyes. The fans whirred, stirring the thick night air ...

"You can't read my thoughts by staring at me," remarked Rupa without looking up.

Embarrassed, the young Inspector rose from his seat and pretended to yawn. He wandered out into the hallway, chatting with the police guards.

"Do you think we can we trust him?" Mahit asked Rupa, in a low voice, when they were alone.

"Anaan would want us to see his notebooks," she replied, not actually answering Mahit's question.

She did not know that answer. Not yet.

She twirled her red-jewel necklace, apparently lost in thought.

She was deep in thought, but she was not lost.

An hour later, the three of them walked into the hallway to stretch their legs.

The Inspector and Mahit avoided asking Rupa what she had read in the notebooks so far.

The open windows offered a light breeze.

A second class of policemen had arrived, mingling with the blue-uniformed constables. They were dressed in tweeds and white collars, like Daniel, like young lawyers, and they spoke low, in staccato sentences.

One of them came and handed Daniel a note and left.

"A Bayes moment," said Daniel, after he had read the note.

"More data.

"Here is word from our colleagues in Oslo. Professor Matthiesen has spent the past six months in a cabin in the Skogshorn forests. No human contact. They trekked up into the hills to interview him at length. It's a dead end.

"We can strike him from our list.

"Now we can revise our theory, what? We are closer to accuracy already!"

As they made their way back into Anaan Warinda's rooms, three maids stepped past, carrying a cleaning cart down the stairs.

"I stayed there," said Rupa to one of the maids.

Rupa pointed to a circular insignia on one of the maid's apron.

It read:

Strangers' Home for Asiatics, Africans and South Sea Islanders

"We lived in a room on the third floor," said Rupa to the maid, a tall, garrulous West Indian her own age.

"For a month. With the *ayahs*. When I first came over."

"'Tis a rough neighborhood," said the tall maid, speaking in a thick accent.

"Kind people. The *ayahs* are most generous." The maid nodded and smiled

"One day soon, Miss," she said. "I'll have me own place."

"Did Professor Warinda leave anything in his trash? Notes, or such?" Rupa asked her.

The maid answered 'No,' but she was a bad liar.

Minutes later, Daniel asked two of his colleagues to check the bins.

Cutaways:
The Battle Of Tirah Followed By A Polite Conversation

*The Khalifa's plan of attack appears to have been
complex and ingenious. It was, however, based on an
extraordinary miscalculation of the power of modern weapons;
with the exception of this cardinal error,
it is not necessary to criticize it ...*

— WINSTON CHURCHILL,
JOURNALIST, FROM HIS ACCOUNT OF THE BATTLE OF OMDURMAN (1898)

A lone British horseman, Lieutenant Connolly, came riding frantically back down the Samana ridge. His steed could hardly keep upright while switch-backing to and fro down the sandy slope.

The first line of the tribal horde advanced over the crest. The warriors of the Orakzai came shouting, sabres and lances held high.

The Battle of Tirah had begun.

Across the battlefield, a small battery of five Maxim guns opened fire,

In an instant, the young tribal warriors in the front line were cut down. Behind them, their brethren took their place. The phalanx marched forward in a dense mass ...

Calmy, relentlessly, the Maxims blasted an unrelenting rain of fire, wave after wave of mechanical death. Far across the way, their bullets plunged into the sand all around the tribesmen, and exploded in dashed clouds of red dust and splinters. The British were finding the range.

The new weapon was the product of an American inventor Hiram Maxim and, secondarily, the mathematician Charles Babbage, whose theories set the stage for Maxim. The Maxim was a rapid-fire gun of such efficiency that it could fire an unimaginable 600 rounds per minute, a boggling leap in lethality. The Maxims fired automatically, using smokeless powder, without any bolt-action or trigger, ingeniously using the recoil from one shot to load and fire the next shot.

The weapon had been well-proven already, in the Matabele war, although the tribesmen of could not have known that. In one engagement, 50 soldiers fought off 5,000 warriors with just four Maxim guns.

After a phase of early misses, sand-spraying dearly misses, the British gunners zeroed in on the foe host.

Undeterred, the brave defenders of Chakdar, the resolute lancers and archers and swordsmen and cavalry of Malakand kept coming.

Here is how one observer described what came next:

"Bullets were shearing through flesh, smashing and splintering bone; blood spouted from terrible wounds; valiant men were struggling on through a hell of whistling metal, exploding shells, and spurting dust—— suffering, despairing, dying. Such was the first phase of the battle."

Something that the tribesmen could not see was killing row upon row of them. Yet still the next row rose and charged, only to be slaughtered, too, never seeing the face of the enemy.

A second row of warriors appeared, and was struck down.

Then a third wave. Felled.

Then a fourth. Crumpled instantly.

On and on.

The men of the 32nd Field Battery fired the Maxims steadily and stolidly, without hurry or excitement. The ranges were known. It was now a matter of technology.

None can say what those brave tribesmen thought of the unseen hissing death that shredded their comrades with such uncaring efficiency.

None can say because none survived.

By a battlefield quirk, when it was over, one warrior's elbow stood at an angle where he had fallen, upright, so that a forearm was raised, sadly displaying a colorful beaded bracelet, there around the wrist.

"Tirah," said Jaiden.

"Five hundred Englishmen slaughter twelve thousand Khyber tribesmen.

"That is what the Germans want from you. The next weapon."

"I can't do that," said Anaan.

"They think you can."

Anaan studied the postcard which Jaiden handed to him It was a depiction of the battle. It displayed a black and white etching of men in traditional poses. All the heroes were British.

The enemy depicted there were his people.

They did not look like that.

Anaan handed the postcard back.

"If that fool Curzon is made Viceroy ..." warned Jaiden.

"It's nothing to do with me," protested Anaan.

"It is your countrymen who will go to war. Wanting freedom. Only to be butchered."

The parlor where the two men conversed was dominated by two very large Oriental rugs, a note-filled chalkboard and two large, framed pieces. One, a map of India and the second a print of *The Gross Clinic*, by the American painter, Thomas Akins.

"Did America wait politely for King George to wake up one morning," argued Jaiden, "and decide to grant them independence? No. No, he didn't."

Anaan said nothing. He was no longer engaged.

"At the very least," continued Jaiden, "don't give your ideas to the Germans. Babu! Is she really all that good?

"It's not like we have a deep bench of other great thinkers. Other world-class mathematicians.

"After you, who is there? Who is there to even understand the work you are doing?

"Who?"

Return To Trinity College:
Secrets Of The Notebooks

At midnight, a half-dozen constables escorted a kitchen worker, dressed in white aprons, into the rooms. He wheeled a small cart. "Try this," said Summerscale, as he offered Rupa and Mahit two pewter bowls, cold to the touch. Spoons protruded from the bowls.

"What is it?" asked Rupa.

"You turn up your nose at English food," said Daniel Summerscale. "Here's a treat even you cannot refuse. It will cool you off.

"Umm. What is it called?"

"Ice cream. I ordered it up from the kitchens."

Rupa tasted it, carefully.

"What flavor is that?" asked Mahit.

"Yours is chocolate. Hers is vanilla."

"Hah! She's the one who loves chocolate."

He indicated Rupa, who seemed to be enjoying the vanilla well enough.

Rupa took a biscuit in the shape of a cone that lay on the cart and scooped the ice cream into it. She took a bite.

She laughed. She ate the entire bowl.

"Thank you," she said to Daniel.

"Got it."

Rupa's announcement caught Summerscale napping in the red leather chair beneath the Eakins print.

Mahit shook his head and peered at the clock. It was just past midnight.

She had so far gone through half of the row of Anaan Warinda's notebooks.

Rupa stood and stretched her hands out, arms wide.

She picked up a piece of foolscap covered in her own writing to show her companions.

"There seem to be two layers of code, one linguistic and one mathematical.

"It's a seven-shift Caesar Code," Rupa explained. "You shift the letters seven down ... it seems to make sense.

"You find a lot of pure mathematics. Number theory, infinite series, that sort of thing.

"Then one entire notebook seems devoted to equalities. Adventures in equalities."

Her two companions regarded her blankly.

"He is relating one mathematical expression to another. I don't really understand it. But this may be what you're hoping for..."

She wrote this on the blackboard:

The coded version: **lzakp pbrjb aqgfj zmtrc vprvq pbiwl pwjoq**

Tamil: **Otticaivu illāmal itu payaṉaṟṟatu**

Hindi: **singaronist ke saath yah bikree hai**

English: **Without synchronization this is useless.**

"Synchronization?" asked Mahit.

"It could mean many things," said Rupa. She shrugged.

She showed them one of Anaan's notebook pages.

"He considers fluid dynamics in this one.

"Apparently, fluid dynamics as they affect an underwater war vessel.

"These here ... seem to be for, moving bombs. Motion-propelled water bombs. He calls them *dhatu machhalee* at one point. See? See here?"

"That exchange that you have translated," asked Summerscale sharply. "With whom was Warinda communicating?"

To answer, Rupa wrote on the chalkboard a five-letter name, first in code, then in Tamil. Then, as she was about to return it to its original language, German —

"HEY! *Hey you!*" came a shout from outside.

A loud clatter exploded on the lawns below the windows.

A hue and cry rose from outside .

They heard heavy steps running down the stairs, joining the commotion on the lawns.

A string of cursing and huffing and whistle-blowing suggested that a pursuit was underway —

Daniel and Mahit both rushed down the stairs and out on the lawn. "Light the perimeters!" called Daniel.

Something told Rupa to hang back.

She heard someone at the door.

She hid behind a bookcase.

She still held the chalk in her hand.

A figure appeared in the doorway.

It was a woman ... and she was stalking something.

Silent, deliberate, the woman moved with purpose. She knew what she wanted.

She wants the notebooks –

The woman stepped into the light. Aquiline features gave her an almost hawk-like aspect. Her eyes were piercing and quick – the eyes of a raptor.

She saw Rupa and rushed.

"Wo sind sie?" she demanded —

"Where are they?" Contempt poisoned her words.

"Come, tell me, *dunkelhautige* –"

She reached, to grab Rupa by the neck –

Rupa twisted the woman's body as she advanced, flipping her from the hallway into the study.

Rupa fisted the hand with the chalk in it and blasted the woman across the jaw.

The blow was unexpected and sprawled the German-speaking intruder backwards, toppling over the desk –

Rupa scrambled to follow her –

Landing cannily on her feet, the woman stepped out of the large open arched window and leapt onto the small balcony –

She vaulted over the railing —

"Hey! Stop! Stop her — "

Rupa called and waved for the constables, but they were spread too thin across the lawn headed towards St Mary's chapel, looking for then phantom danger that had decoyed the intruder's approach.

"Catch her! Over there — she's near the trees!" Rupa called out the window.

But the burglar had disappeared in the shadows.

When order had been restored and her two colleagues had returned from chasing the decoy, Rupa turned to face young Special Inspector Summerscale.

"Who was that woman?" Rupa demanded, and by that she most clearly meant,

Tell me everything you know, or I quit.

Mystery Of The Notebooks // Trinity College // Daniel's Confession

I see something you can't see.

— MITCHELL BURGESS

The trio sat at the tea cart pulled into Anaan's rooms. The surgeon, Dr. Samuel Gross, glared down at them from Eakins' painting. Like them, Dr. Gross had found the path to the truth to be a winding road.

"I am part of a ... singular agency. Not the regular Metropolitan police force," said Daniel Summerscale

"A task force with a different directive.

"A shadow war is already being fought. Not just here, but all across Europe. Asia as well. We operate in that arena. It is a deadly game.

"We believe that London is a stage. A stage upon which the dramas of the global – the rise and fall of empires — are being played out.

"The houses of the West are sinking, and breaking apart as they sink, in their slow decline. The empires of the Orient rise.

"Science and technology have now joined the battlefield. Modern warcraft will be unrecognizable from past wars.

"The Minie bullet you saw in the American Civil War, the Gatling, the new trains bringing thousands to the front line, to be slaughtered by the new machines — these are just the beginning. Aviation. Airplanes with bombs. Battleships like cities.

"I have seen with my own eyes the realities of the new warfare.

"Since Omdurman, since Tirah, powerful forces seek the science behind the new technologies for themselves. Nations who lost in the scramble for Africa have vowed not to be left out again.

"It is a deadly race for the new technology.

"Warinda, rightly or wrongly, was seen as a rainmaker in this landscape of new thinking.

"This, I fear, may have been his undoing.

"The women you encountered —- her name is Emmaline Krauss. It is she who has bewitched Anaan. Whether she was going to sell his secrets to Krupp or Medici or to the Russians, we don't yet know.

"Our night has been well-spent. We are closer to knowing the truth.

"Let's get you two out of the line of fire, shall we? Your family wanted you home by dawn, Miss Rupa."

"But we haven't solved the problem," said Rupa. "Who killed Anaan? Why? What did they get from him? I have more notebooks to — "

"We're closer than you think," answered the Inspector. "You have been a tremendous help."

Pulling Rupa's jacket from the coat-rack, Mahid accidentally knocked the rack over.

As it toppled and clattered to the floor, an object hidden in the wooden post was knocked loose.

It was long and thin.

Rupa picked it up and found it light to the touch.

She carried it to the desk. It was a roll of parchment,

She carefully unwrapped it.

Notations and labels had been marked on a very thin roll of paper.

"It's a parchment overlay," said Rupa. "We use these at my engineering firm."

Moving slowly, she carried the parchment and placed it over the wall-mounted map of India.

Using the frame as a reference point, the three of them taped the parchment on top of the map of India.

Rupa made small adjustments until ...

A perfect fit.

The overlay exactly displayed numbers and equations and ratios over corresponding Indian states, cities, rivers, garrisons and major ports.

"We are looking at the plans for an Indian uprising," said Daniel, "in the form of a map."

It would be a great war, one fought on many fronts.

"This corresponds to some of the notations I saw," said Rupa, inspecting a large panel of mathematics pasted over Madras.

"This ratio. Here. 24:1. It refers to the Raj. Twenty-four Indians for every Englishman."

"Huh. Looks like Mumbai goes down first," commented Daniel. "That's just what I would do."

"Here." Rupa pointed to figures dotting the northern states. "These same ratios crop up ... in Anaan's notes," she continued, "when he's discussing an iteration of Lanchester's Law."

"Lanchester's Law'?" asked Daniel.

"Differential equations," replied Rupa. "Two opposing forces in a violent confrontation. It's low math, for someone like Anaan."

"This is the work of Jaiden and his lot," mumbled Mahit. Rupa started to protest, then stopped.

"Surely these here mark the British garrisons," said Daniel, bending down to look at the marked sites along the southern coasts. "Pondicherry ... Kerala ...Gujarat ..."

"He's gauging how much manpower will it take to overthrow each garrison. And which weapons they will need to overcome the Maxims and cannons.

"Look the ports. He's notched the British ships in the fleet. Not very accurately, I'd say.

"Mathematical probabilities to overthrow the Raj," concluded Daniel wryly.

"A numerical look at a civil war."

Mahit let out a low whistle. His face held the expression of one who has seen the supernatural.

"The veil between the worlds is thin," said that worthy, cryptically. "I can almost feel Anaan here. With us."

The comment lingered in the summer air, suddenly gone heavy.

"It's been a long night." Daniel clapped his hands.

He signaled to someone in the doorway.

"Well done. Thank you, Rupa. Thank you, Mahit."

A carriage rolled up to the transom of Whewell House's stairwell. Two of Daniel's colleagues got out.

"We'll take it from here."

As they parted, Rupa gave Daniel an envelope.

"What's this?"

"Give it to the Coroner," she replied as the carriage began the trip to the train station.

"It might help."

"My cousin Dargai died at Tahir," said Rupa when she and Mahit were alone, on the train back to London.

"His name was Dargai. He was just a boy.

"I made a bracelet for him. For luck … in battle …"

"These are epic times," said Mahit carefully. "God's times. We must choose our path carefully."

"We now have dual loyalties," said Rupa worriedly.

"Daniel's agency is looking to dismantle Jaiden. Our countryman."

"If Jaiden seeks to bomb women and children, like the Irish, he is no countryman of mine," concluded Mahit grimly.

"Three of Anaan's notebooks are missing," said Rupa.

"I may know where to find them."

Pause.

“You should ask your Father,” added Mahit. “He’ll know what to do.”

Cutaway Scene Aboard The India Princess
Ten Years Earlier

"Are you hiding?" asked the little girl.

The slim young man crammed in the narrow space between the steam-ship's black funnels looked down at his inquisitor. Winds blew the salt air and ruffled his hair.

"Yes. Yes, I am hiding," he replied.

Rupa, aged seven, took this in stride. The slim young man was in plain sight, so it was not a very good job of hiding.

"Would you like some chocolate?" she asked.

She raised her left hand, which held a half-eaten piece of chocolate, wrapped in tinfoil.

"Yes," said the young man. "I would."

With solemn attention to detail, Rupa snapped off a reasonably-sized piece of her chocolate bar and carefully handed it to him.

"You're very kind," he added, appreciatively.

The young man's narrow shoulders were barely covered by a ragged, once-elegant ivory-colored woolen sweater. He had rolled up the sleeves. Neither the sweater nor his slacks were a match for the winter winds of the Arabian Sea. Crammed between the black-painted funnels. It was a snug hiding place, one where passenger might enjoy a clear view of the mighty waters, out of eyesight from fellow passengers.

"This is delicious," he said.

The *Princess of India* was not primarily a passenger ship. The Belfast vessel was a fast merchant ship, which made the passage carrying 2500 tons of cargo for the P& O line.

"What do they eat in London?" the girl asked.

"Lots of potatoes," he conjectured. "Roast beef. Some soybeans, I hear."

The pair savored the chocolate. They stood on the tilting deck and watched the rolling seas together.

Waves rose and fell, rising, collapsing and re-forming, each different, on each rise.

"My name is Anaan, by the way," the young man said. "Anaan Warinder."

"I am Rupashana," the girl answered. "Rupashana Lal Pyradhakrishnan."

"That is a beautiful name," said Anaan. "But it's too long. Might I just call you Ruby? Ruby Pi?"

The ship gracefully rose and fell. The sounds of the sea washed over them.

"All right," she answered.

His stomach gurgled loudly.

"Sorry. That's rude of me." He explained, "hepatic amoebiasis. Stomach condition."

The Arabian Sea lies west of India, south of the Suez, north and east of Africa, and two thousand nautical miles closer to Europe than the Cape of Good Hope.

Anaan gestured towards a boy standing across the way, on the lower deck, standing against the staircase. He was watching them. He had almost the same features as Rupa. He did not seem to blink, or waver in any way.

"Is that your brother?"

"Cousin," she replied. "Vardan."

Anaan waved to cousin Vardan, with no visible response.

Far north and east, much further than they could see, lay the Persian Gulf. The *Princess* would swing west and south, to skirt the mouth of the Persian Gulf, then follow the Oman coast to Djobouti, then Eritrea, then enter the Red Sea and then the Suez Canal.

The second leg of the journey, to London, would follow.

"Do you know, Rupa," ventured Anaan, "I believe there might be a way to measure the height of those waves."

The longer one looks out at the ocean waters, the more complex become the many motions and currents, the collective and individual repeating patterns.

"I doubt it," said Rupa. "They're moving too fast.

"See how they rise up just for a second, and then sink back down?" she pointed out.

"No," said Anaan, "but I mean in theory. Mathematically.

"What if we were measuring them from behind?" he continued. "We could see the stages of motion more ... more distinctly. In continuous stages. Like Muybridge ..."

"But there is no fixed correlative, no reference point, you're thinking." Anaan said, answering his own unstated question.

"But still," he corrected himself yet again, "the crest and trough could be measured before the wave collapses.

"I think your chocolate has helped me see it clearly."

Rupa nodded, as if that same thing happened to her, too. She would come to understand that Anaan often talked to himself, and that this internal dialogue was how he worked things out, and that she just happened to be present.

It was a long voyage, and the two would become good companions.

"How would that go?" the little girl asked.

"The math. How would that work?"

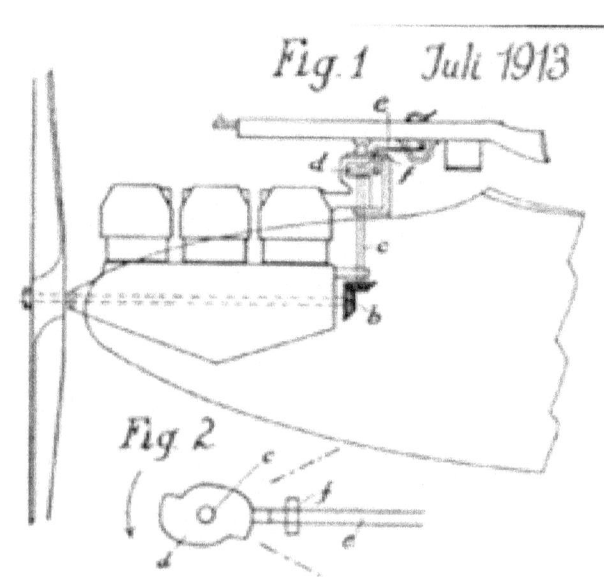

Climax // *Fight At The Wharfs*

"Danger," he said.

His eyes took on a strange, bright, blank look.

— RICHARD PRESTON

T o sleepy Mahit's surprise and disapproval, Rupa requested that the carriage driver take them to Temple Pier, Wharf Six. The time was 3:20 a.m.

"Most of the world is asleep," he complained.

"I think I know where the three notebooks are," she declared.

This explanation seemed reasonable to Mahit.

In the carriage, Mahit hummed softly as the engines churned and the train rolled northward. It was a popular song that he hummed, "Asleep in the Deep," and while the melody was pretty, the lyrics referred to persons who unhappily found themselves in the ocean's darkest reaches, fathoms down.

The Strangers' Home for Asiatics, Africans and South Sea Islanders is a free-standing sturdy brick building on West India Dock Road, in the Limehouse district.

The women who ran the Home welcomed Asian sailors, black long-shoremen, ayahs, the Indian nannies abandoned by their British families, and other orphans of the docks.

When their carriage arrived at Wharf Six, Rupa and Mihat stepped cautiously out, into the fog and cobblestone and the eerie quiet.

A few stragglers moved along the empty streets. A drunk serenaded one of the ships lined up along the wharfs. Dawn was not far off.

Rupa and Mahit crossed the broad avenue and entered. The lobby was all high ceilings and bright colors. The furniture was modest, well-worn but clean. The desk clerk called her supervisor, and it took some convincing before they knocked discreetly on the second-story bedroom.

"Me back foot!" exclaimed the sleepy young woman when she opened the door to see Rupa and Mahid.

This was the maid they had met earlier in the night, in the staircases.

"Hello, Miss!"

Rupa apologized for the hour and explained that she wished to look through the hand-sized notepads that had been thrown out of Professor Warinda's rooms. Rupa had noticed them among the knick-knacks and discards on the cleaning cart. The police had scoured the trash bins and found nothing. Rupa was hoping the maids might have kept one.

The young maid at first protested, insisting that they were empty, and of no use to anyone, until Rupa was able to assure her that she had done nothing wrong. Mahit paid her handsomely for the three hand-sized note pads which she had preserved from Anaan Warinda's rooms.

Rupa and Mahit huddled on the front porch of the Asian Sailors' Home to inspect the pads. "Yes," said Rupa. "They look empty, but he stashed these separately for a reason — "

The eccentric mathematician had scattered his notes, like a squirrel scattering its acorn treasure. Some he had apparently hidden in the trash cans. Rupa removed several pages that had been carefully folded and hidden in the pads' backing. She placed them in her jacket pocket.

"This may be Anaan's most recent correspondences," Rupa told Mahit as they descended the porch steps to return to the carriage. "I can break them down as soon I get home …"

It was just then that fortune changed everything.

A small group was walking towards them in the fog.

Odd, in the dead of night …

Something about the way the members of the group stood relative to one another, the way they all moved, something in the postures, was wrong.

They came close.

Now Rupa could see four stout men and three girls –little girls, no m ore than nine or ten, girls who should be safe in bed surrounded by dolls and puppies — being dragged along a desolate London pier.

A light mist played at their ankles.

The lamplight caught one girl's tear-streaked face: the stricken expression which every man or woman who has ever lived would know … the look of fear and hopeless panic.

"*Madad karana!*" cried the brave girl, looking straight at Rupa –

With a cry, Rupa threw herself at the men, intending to break their grip on their young captives –

"*Krpaya hamaaraee madad karen!*" sobbed the girl in a heart-breaking voice.

"Help! Help! Help us!"

The little girl pulled away, trying to wrest free —

Rupa smashed down at the captors' hands, trying to break the grip on the girl's wrists –

Rupa was grabbed roughly around the neck.

She had never felt such deadly strength.

He's going to kill me —

Rupa kicked wildly and twisted free of the grip.

She swung a third blow as hard as she could —

One of the girls fell away, freed.

Now Mahit joined the fray and struck with the billy-club., dropping one of the villains —

All hell broke loose.

Rupa thought she heard scuffling shoes and shouting in a strange language as a second party joined the fray —

Now the freed girl returned, screaming like a banshee, to help her sisters, —

Rupa felt hands and fingers clawing at her jacket.

Then – surprisingly, if any had been conscious enough to be surprised — a *third* group joined the melee.

Whistles and calls of "Police!" and "Stop!" filled the air.

Was that a gunshot?

For a long moment, Temple Pier at Wharf Six at was witness to the kind of primitive, eye-gouging, hand-to-hand combat that has been part of humankind since the days of Zaphath and Prahasta.

Rupa lashed out and struck a face –

A man grabbed her and lifted her.

She felt something in her arm snap –

"Lay down your arms!" she heard Daniel command, dimly aware that she must now be dreaming.

Then, whether it was the late night and lack of sleep, or the hours spent studying the intricacies of mathematics in in forced calm, or whether it was rage at the living memory of her slaughtered cousin and closest ancestor ... Rupa surged, wolflike.

She was no longer civilized.

With uncanny strength, she broke free and lunged for the throat of the burly kidnapper who was choking her.

When they found her, she had both hands clutched tightly around the dead man's windpipe —

Hospital Room

*Indians in London were not only building the
city, but also shaping the course of the
nationalist movement in India.*

— Chatterjee,' Indians in London'

Be very careful with this story, Mister Waters. It bites.

—Thomas Perry

I n the hospital room, Mother showered Rupa with all of the family's fondest pet names — *Ruby Pi, Rupaji, Rupimandaji, Rupichandra, Rubaiyat Chocolate* – to invoke a safer, calmer time, Rupa's childhood, in the hope it would protect her daughter from this wicked world.

A white cloth sling held Rupa's left arm immobile. The lower part of the arm was in a cast. Purple bruising colored her forehead and upper cheek. A bandage hid one ear.

The hubbub created by the extended Pyradhakrishnan family and friends overwhelmed the hospital corridors.

Deferential to the visitors, blue-uniformed constables cleared a path for young Special Inspector Daniel Summerscale. He, too, was bandaged. He walked with the help of a crutch.

When he and Rupa were alone, he turned on her angrily.

"What in the hell were you thinking?

"You attacked four armed criminals with nothing but your bare hands. At four o'clock in the morning. On a deserted Pier. If I hadn't been there ..."

Vardan knocked on the window, shooting Daniel a warning glare.

"What did you think was going to happen?" Daniel demanded of Rupa.

"What did actually happen?" Rupa asked.

Daniel took a seat, slowly, minding his leg and his crutch.

"Well. When you decided to confront the smugglers – they were Portuguese, by the way, not Turks — the *Thyssen* who were following you saw an opportunity to grab the missing notes from you. From your jacket pocket.

"Then we swooped in on both lots. Had the entire pier surrounded.

"Did you know those girls? Did you know they were going be there?"

"No," answered Rupa. "But as soon as I saw them ... I knew I had to get them away from those men."

"The girls were orphans," reported Daniel. "Apparently arrived on the Mirabelle, hoping to be adopted. When the adopting families never showed, the smugglers saw their chance. The Portageese waited until everyone was gone to transport the girls —

"You are insanely brave, you know. Never seen the like."

"So," said Rupa. "I was bait?"

"No, no, that's not the case – well, yes. I suppose you were."

Rupa combed her fingers through her hair where it met the bandage, trying to get it smoothed down.

"Was there a gun shot?" asked Rupa. "Or did I imagine it?"

Daniel hesitated.

"An operative," he replied, "who sometimes calls himself Farquhar was there. I saw him last in a kitchen alley, in Istanbul.

"It was he who decorated my forearm.

"I took the opportunity to repay him.

"He will not be visiting Sultanahmet again."

Eshaan and Narinder waved to Rupa through the glass. Rupa waved back.

"And the Coroner?" Rupa asked.

"He has filed his preliminary report. It seems you were right. Anaan Warinda died of an acute onset of chronic dysentery. *Hepatic amoebiasis.* Apparently, a long-term condition. He was not poisoned, after all."

Daniel moved a pitcher of water closer to her on the bedside table.

"What will happen to the girls?" he asked.

"They and three of the *ayahs* are already part of Little Mumbai."

Special Inspector Summerscale waved to Eshaan.

"This government owes you a debt we can scarcely repay."

"You owe me nothing, Daviesite," Rupa replied.

"Robinite!" He laughed. "Class of '91."

"Well, it is I who have a gift for you, Special Inspector, and Robinite," said Rupa. "A memento."

Moving awkwardly, she reached into the drawer in the table beside her and handed him a folded piece of foolscap. It was a page from one of the notebooks.

Here is what she had written on it:

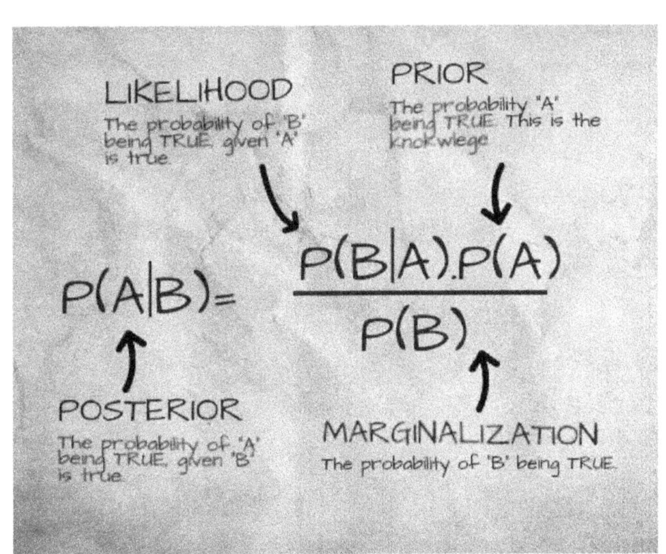

"Ah," said The Inspector. "The Bayes Theorem."

He read and re-read it, as though committing it to memory.

"I take it to heart."

Ending: The Minister's Visit

Help thy brother's boat across, and lo!
thine own has reached the shore.

—Hindu proverb

U p the street, the unmistakable clatter of hooves clomping on cobblestone suggested that a visitor of some stature was arriving in Little Mumbai.

A clamor of horses and carriages advanced up the quiet neighborhood tucked off High Street, Croydon.

The procession came to a halt outside the Pyradhakrishnan family residence.

Curious neighbors crowded around to see the carriage door open.

Out walked a Cabinet member and Minister. Knighted in later life, his was a face and a gait and a voice that would one day be well-known to history. Today we shall use only the initials WSC.

This was a man of unforced charm, a universal man such as one rarely encounters, smart, demanding, often amused, self-deprecating yet supremely confident of himself and his nation, all at the same time.

He held a cigar in one hand. He made an old-fashioned, regal-style wave with the other. Daniel Summerscale attended, making introductions.

Walking to the front door, WSC held out his hand to Father.

"I am pleased to meet you, sir. And you must be Raayani. Mother of Rupa. Aha!" Mother bowed, despite herself.

Swirling around the Minister and onto the front lawn, a team of tidy men had emerged from a large wagon. They set up a large, wheeled apparatus, wood and metal, painted white, with large lettering that announced, "Ice Cream." Cranks and colored bottles of syrup and open half-barrels were visible along the top of the cart, with thick-walled metal trays for ice beneath.

"As modern a machine as you will find at Brixton!" announced the Minister. "A token of our esteem."

"Ah! There she is!"

Rupa appeared in the doorway.

"Chocolate for you, I understand," he said to Rupa. "How jolly. Where is Mahit? I was told to ask for Mahit."

Ice cream cones were served to all.

The Minister raised his ice cream cone to salute Rupa, Mahit, Father, Mother, the entire Pyradhakrishnan family, their many friends and neighbors, the ex-pat community as a whole, and India at large.

"I am hopeful that this morning will show our solidarity," he said. "Our gratitude. Our brotherhood.

"You, you friends of England, you have come from the subcontinent to give shape to modern Britain. Truly.

"The Commonwealth thrives because of you.

"The bonds of empire endure.

"We demonstrate once again how strong are the ties between our peoples. England! India! God save the Queen!" He smiled at this last exclamation.

"I take my leave."

When the Minister and his entourage had retreated, Daniel sat in the big chair across from the pink sofa, where Rupa sat.

"We caught up with the German woman. Miss Krause. In Marseilles. She was on her way back to the Rhineland, via the long route.

"She had a few choice things to say about you.

"It she who ... persuaded Anaan. He was apparently under her spell.

"My job is done. For now.

"Thanks to you, we know what killed him. A childhood disease that he never got over.

"Also thanks to you, we have a pretty clear idea of what Anaan was working on during those last months."

Daniel did not mention Jaiden, or synchronization, or the map of the Indian rebellion against Britain.

Does he suspect ...?

Daniel handed Rupa a book.

She opened it.

She read the title page:

An Essay towards solving a Problem in the Doctrine of Chances

She read the author's name:

Thomas Bayes

She read the date of publication:

1763

A first edition.

"Thank you," said Rupa. "This is … most thoughtful. You are most kind, Carthusian."

Daniel smiled, pleased at her reaction.

"Perhaps you'd like to perform a tribal celebration," he suggested. "A dance of some kind."

She smiled and nodded.

"Yes. Yes, I would. You can join in. It is a ritual that involves the sacrifice of a young Englander …"

Fragrances from the clattering kitchen filled the air.

Was that saffron?

Had Mother found those Malabar peppercorns at the market?

Rupa could smell roasted poultry cooking, its salted skin turning golden brown. She imagined the platter of over-buttered, braised red potatoes and sprinkled green parsley on which the poultry would be presented.

"The Mathematical Society lads have tried to follow your lead," Daniel told her. "They are determined to chart out the entire contents of Anaan's notebooks. Page by page. They want to run some of their translations by you, when you're up to it."

"Of course," Rupa assented.

Daniel rose. He said good-bye, with a bow.

Miss Rupalshara Lal Pyradhakrishnan corrected her posture, as she sat straight, there on the pink sofa, in the parlor of her family's home.

The screen door closed.

Now she could detect lighter smells in the air, like the oil and vinegar that was sprinkled on the salads, and herb garnishes, lovingly chopped and arrayed around the platters

It was Saturday. Dinner was served at noon.

The neighborhood outside hummed with life, football games in the grass, easy conversations.

London seemed intact.

India, half a world distant, seemed intact.

She had not mentioned to Special Inspector Summerscale the several sheets of Anaan's notes which she had withheld.

There would be time to understand them, in their full import, later.

Rupa knew well the accounts of the slaughter at Tirah.

She had listened, too, to Danile's warning about the new and monstrous face of war.

She began to understand Anaan's dilemma, the choice he had been forced to make between his ancestral home and his adopted home, between Tamil Nadu and Surrey. Between India and England.

One day, Rupa, too would have to choose sides.

But for today, her arm was mending. Her arm was mending, the ice cream was cold and sweet, the mystery of Anaan Warinda had been cracked open, just a little, and she was sitting on a comfortable couch, reading a first edition of a most learned book.

From the kitchen, Mother called for Narinder to set the table.

Rupa took a deep breath. Were those berries she could smell, half-floating in the bullion? She closed her eyes and thought of the bowls of steaming stew and spice-soaked noodles on the good ceramic plates, mounds of saffron rice and thick pieces of bread which served so well to soak up the rich gravy.

The family was gathering.

Dinner would be ready soon.

TOM'S NOTES

I modeled my character Anaan Warinda on the well-known Indian mathematician, Srinivasa Ramanujan. He famously reached out from his village in India to disseminate his home-made proofs, and was brought to England to study, before dying young

Bayes' Rule seems to be one of the more significant and useful theories in mathematics. Deceptively so. Bayes Rule is central to all decision-making ... how tightly should you hold on to your view, and how much should you update your view based on new information

A wonderful book by Sharon Bertsch McGrayne entitled *The Theorem that Would Not Die* explains how the theorem "cracked the enigma code, hunted down Russian submarines and emerged triumphant from two centuries of controversy." This is a full and engaging explanation of a very powerful and elegant idea which I have presented in the crudest form possible.

How to attack any problem ...

The author feels strongly that you should be a Bayesian.

Under Bayes' theorem, no theory is perfect. Rather, it is a work in progress, always subject to further refinement and testing.

In my battle scene, I have replaced the Battle of Tirah with the Battle of Omdurman. This is a different (Anglo-Egyptian) yet similar battle of the same era. I use it because Omdurman even more dramatically demonstrates the new era of 'machine death,' as its chronicler, young Winston Churchill, called it. You will never read anything quite like Churchill's account t of that one-sided encounter.

In writing the Tirah battle scene, I wanted to somehow get across the idea that Dargai and his friends were fighting or expecting to fight a traditional, honorable, fair combat for bragging rights to a piece of territory – more like a really harsh football match — and not the long-distance annihilation that marked the start of a new era of warfare.

There will be much more to say regarding The Raj in later stories, which take Rupa and her family deep into the forge of empires (the struggle between Britain and India, that is)

Regarding the story's two references to passion intersecting with mathematics, these have always been an uneasy mix. Here is a vivid tale from the history of math.

In Paris, 1789, Evariste Galois was not yet twenty. Like other young men, he was passionate

Evariste Galois was one of the most brilliant mathematicians to walk the earth. While his proofs were often sloppy , the teenaged Evariste was able to determine a condition for a polynomial to be solvable by radicals, solving a problem standing for over 300 years. He lobbed papers on continued fractions and polynomial equations into the mathematical councils of the Academy of Sciences, raging if his ideas were doubted.

On June 2, 1832, this brilliant young mathematician got into an argument over a woman. Emotions rose. Perceived insults were traded in a heated exchanged. A challenge to a duel of honor was issued. The challenge was accepted.

The next morning saw the two young duelists square off.

At point blank range, each was armed with a pistol.

Each fired.

Galois was pierced through and through by a ball from his opponent.

He was taken to the hospital Cochin and died in two hours.

Galois was dead.

Fortunately, on the night before, in some kind of premonition, he had scribbled down every idea in his head all of his theories. With the mathematics, he included these heartbreaking notes:

I beg patriots and my friends not to reproach me for dying
Oh! why die for such a trivial thing?
Pardon for those who have killed me, they are of good faith

Young Galois' work is still with us. "He explained the basic mathematics of symmetry," recounts Ian Stewart in his book "Significant Figures." Galois' theories have proven invaluable to scholars investigating group theory. which recurs often in algebra.

Beware the coming together of youth, passion and mathematical theory.

Here is one of the math consultant's clarification on my ill-considered use of the term 'vector' in the train scene:

> *It sounds a bit strange to say that a vector is moving since a vector does not really live in our "real" space but in some abstract mathematical space. Maybe you could use the word "momentum" instead of vector of speed and force. Momentum is still a vector, but it's (velocity x mass) and even if it is still a vector it is used in the physical jargon to mean "something heavy that moves very fast ..."*

2. Blue Moon Over the Mogollons

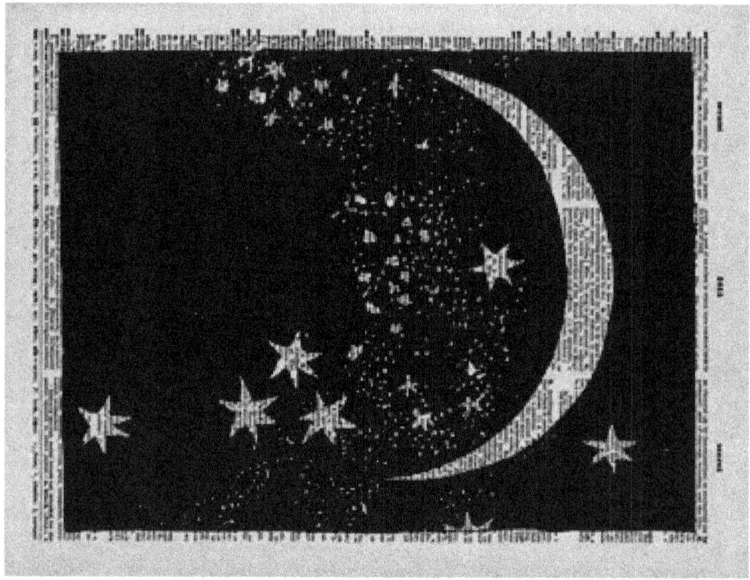

SYNOPSIS: A poker game, a special rifle, and a family on the verge of drastic change. New Mexico Territories, 1877

Card Game #1
More Than It Seems

— SALLIE SCHILDHAUER, A BRIEF HISTORY OF THE NAVIGATORS

"Seven shuffles," said Ma, looking young in her gingham dress. "Seven's my lucky number."

Smiles around the card table.

"Both my kids were born on the seventh day of the month."

The young mother nodded proudly towards her chatty 14-year-old daughter, Casey, and her sullen older child, Johnny.

It takes seven shuffles to clear a deck of cards. Seven ordinary shuffles mix the cards thoroughly, so that neither the dealer nor any of the players can know what card is coming, and when.

It was a card game of good will and fellowship in a Silver City saloon in the shadow of the wild Mogollons. Dealer's Choice. The deal passed after each game.

"Five card draw," Ma announced. "Deuces wild."

The young mother, Margery, finished the sixth shuffle, then the seventh. She was not particularly, dexterous, and two cards flipped out of place. She reassembled the deck and smoothed its edges.

Ma dealt cards to each player around the table. *One, two, three ...*

"Almanac says a Blue Moon starts tomorrow," said the lawyer, Aynsley, as the cards were being dealt. Like most lawyers, he enjoyed the sound of his own voice.

"Ooooo," cooed his wife, sitting nearby.

"Interestingly enough," continued Aynsley, "the Blue Moon phenomenon is a result of Krakatoa. The volcano. The Polynesian volcano. It spread ash fifty miles into the stratosphere, you see. Billions of particles, each less than a micron in size. It acts as filter, scattering red light. Turning the moon blue. In appearance, that is. The moon itself is unchanged."

Aynsley turned in four cards.

"Oooooo," commented Mrs. Aynsley. "Can you imagine?"

"Yes. It is sometimes called the 'betrayer's moon,' because it betrays our usual perceptions. Refraction. The air itself acts as a prism. No two of us see the same color, you know. The moon itself does not change, just the ways we experience it."

Morgan, the militia man, took three cards.

"I never knowed that," said the farmer, Wills. "I seen blue moons, but I never knowed why."

The farmer turned in two cards.

"Hey, this peanut bowl is empty," Casey remarked to Angie, the sweet-faced saloon waitress. Angie walked behind the bar and emerged with a jar. She refilled all the peanut bowls on each table.

"Thanks," said Casey.

The reference to 'peanut bowl' told the Mother to double her bet.

Ma pushed the chips forward, three blue and three white. Her motions were tentative, nothing bold enough to call attention.

Wills threw in his hand. "I'm out."

"Haw!" said Morgan. He matched Ma's bet, and raised her.

"Ma, can we go soon?" said Casey, fifteen-year-old daughter. "I'm in agony."

The use of the word 'agony' indicated a dearth of Aces yet to be played.

A lackage.

No more Aces.

Stop chasing the royal straight, urged Casey silently. *What are you doing?*

Ma took two cards.

"And what's a fine little family like yours doing in Silver City, in these wild times?" Aynsley asked Ma.

"We're holding a little gun repair clinic tomorrow," answered Ma. "You should come."

"And after that?" asked Mrs. Aynsley.

"We're on our way to Albuquerque. My husband's waiting for us."

"Well, keep an eye out for Apaches and the like between here and Albuquerque," clucked the lawyer's wife. "We've heard of highwaymen."

Ma matched Aynsley's bet. Morgan did the same.

"T'wouldn't be Apache, ma'am," said the farmer, Wills. "Comanche, mebbe. Or jes' plain crooked folks. Lotsa them around."

With a mouthful of peanuts, Casey began to hum, softly. It was Stephen Foster's song, "O' Hard Times, Come No More."

The Stephen Foster song signaled an emergency.

Fold.

Quit the game.

Now!

Ignoring all the signals they had practiced, and reviewed, over and over, Ma raised the bet again. She pushed two handfuls of chips towards the center of the table.

"Whoa!" exclaimed Morgan.

Casey hummed, softly singing the second verse, about wraiths at the door. Ma paid no attention.

Morgan matched the bet.

Aynsley did the same.

"Call."

Ma turned over her cards.

Full house.

Ma won.

She made no move to collect her winnings, Aynsley and Wills chivalrously doing so for her.

"We gotta go," said Casey, standing at her Mother's shoulder, something she had never done.

"One more hand, dear — " protested Ma.

"Do stay, Margery," urged Aynsley. "Give us the chance to win it back — "

"Weren't that much, sir," said Casey. "And we got the clinic tomorrow — "

"She's a grown woman," objected Mrs. Aynsley.

"Did you not hear what I said?"

Casey had turned to face the lawyer's wife directly.

This was an entirely different young woman speaking now.

Behind her, Johnny stood up.

His right hand hovered beside his belt, on the right side, where a bulge in his jacket suggested a holster and pistol.

"No, Casey's right."

Ma excused herself.

"I do get run-down easily.

"Thank you, thank you all. Good night."

"My my! Tempers do flare in these times!" complained Mrs. Aynsley. "What a strange way for that little family to behave ..."

"Must be the Blue Moon, dear." Mr. Aynsley shuffled.

"Nine card stud, gentlemen."

The card game resumed.

The little family retired up the stairs.

Hotel Room Scene 1

It was my personality that decided all this.

— Wu Lihong, quoted by Joseph Kahn

"W*hat was that?*" Casey asked Ma. "You were holding a heart and two spades. Five clubs had already been played. Your chances of success had dropped through the floor — "

"Yes yes, dear," said Ma lightly.

"If you keep ignoring the percentages ... "

"Oh, Case I was just having a little fun — "

Ma tossed the money belt on the bed.

The deed came close behind.

"You've got to talk in complete sentences," admonished Casey. "You need to sound like a schoolteacher."

Ma poured a drink into a small whisky glass and downed it.

"You won three games right in a row!! You can't do that! We agreed!"

Johnny said nothing, but he was listening. Watching Ma.

"Case, the feeling just *took hold* of me — " Ma tried to explain.

"You and your feelings — "

"Well, that's how you two come to get here — "

"MOM! JEEZ! That's *gross*. I can't believe you *said* that — "

Case had counted the money. She had reassembled her notes. She wrote in her journal what had happened, the games, the players, the sequences, the bets, the cards played.

Ma looked at the bottle as if she were ready for another glass. Johnny caught the look and put the bottle away.

"Why can't we just have a normal family?" asked Casey, with a certain depth of feeling, suspecting that even asking the question was a sign of hopelessness.

The question hung in the air like tiny particles of ash, echoes of some distant calamity, too small for the eye to see.

Saloon Gun Repair Clinic

*"I always find myself
instinctively arrayed on the side of the
barbarian, against the powers of
organized civilization."*

— ROBERT E. HOWARD

"Say, did you serve in the *Revolutionary* War?" asked the dexterous young woman, Casey, with a smile.

The trapper, a huge mountain-man dressed in furs, reluctantly gave up a chuckle.

"Gun Cleaning and Repair Clinic" announced the sign in the saloon window, with an addendum "Friday 8 to 4" attached to the top corner.

"No, I did not," he replied. "My grandpa did carry ammo for Clay, at Fort Meigs."

"On the Maumee?" She let out a whistle. "And lived to tell. That's somethin'.

"And was this here his rifle at the time?"

"No. It ain't quite that old ..."

The grouchy trapper's features warmed. He cocked and un-cocked the brand-new hammer.

"Kit Carson used this same model, did you know that?" commented Casey.

The saloon's ample seating was full. Gunmen from all walks of life waited patiently on the sidewalk outside, in a line going down to Yannick's stables.

Casey handed over the long-barreled Hawes squirrel rifle which she had taken apart and put together, cleaned and polished. The weapon gleamed.

The trapper turned the rifle stock over and back to admire the newly-polished wood in the light.

"I did know that. His was never so well-cared as this, I bet."

The trapper removed a bag of coins. He opened the bag and placed five gold coins on the table.

Casey stood up to shake his hand.

"Heard you was good," said the trapper.

"You could charge more, y'know," said the young barkeep, Drew, as he cleaned the table, readying for the next customer.

Casey smiled and shook her head.

A slim, quiet woman not much older than Casey stepped up. Next in line.

She wore overalls and a deep fatigue on her face. She held a sleeping baby with a pink woven cap against her shoulder.

Slowly, she lifted a heavy, elongated leather sling and placed it on the table.

It was a leather rifle pouch, or carrying case.

"Long gun." Casey gave a low whistle.

Casey opened the pouch. She removed a smooth-barreled, wood-grained stock. She took care, checking for shells. Next came a steel barrel, and a telescopic sight. Casey put the weapon together, her fingers moving with practiced speed.

"Ma'am, this here's an Enfield distance rifle. Snider-Enfield. Five fifty-seven. A precision weapon, if I ever saw one." She ran a cleaning rag along the smooth metal barrel.

"The British Army snipers swear by these."

"It's worth more money than all the firearms in this room, put together."

"Not to me, it ain't," answered the young lady. "It belonged to my ex. My new husband, he cain't make it work. Says it's busted.

"He come to tell me that it's either get rid of the rifle or get rid of him. So whatever you can give me, I'll take it."

Three of the 9th Cavalry scouts, over from Fort Stanton, who were waiting their turn, came over to look.

Casey held the Enfield up for them to see. One of the scouts hefted the rifle as Casey removed a booklet, a bottle of oil, and a cleaning rag from the rifle carrying-pouch.

The baby girl in her arms shivered, made a dream sound, and fell back to sleep.

Casey tossed the rifle to her mother. It was a graceful, long-barreled breech-loader. The stock was cross-grained walnut. The block housed an unusual diagonal, downward-sloping firing pin.

Ma cocked the mounted hammer, flipped the breech block lever, and pulled the block back. Twice. She held it to her shoulder and squinted into the sight. Click. She nodded. She tossed it to Johnny. Johnny nodded.

"Well," said Casey, "I can give you half a dozen boxes of Remington shells. Two-two threes. Is that what the new husband shoots? Here's … here's six dollars in cash. An' we got a twenny-dollar marker at the grocery store. There's a little more than four dollars left. I can give you that much. Ain't a fair price for an Enfield."

"That's fine, Miss. We'll take it." Holding the baby tight, the young mother gave Casey a quarter-bow.

"And thank you. I thank you."

The other customers, mostly hard Western men, gathered in the saloon, nursing their weapons, waiting their turn, took note.

"Square deal," commented one of the 9th Cavalry scouts.

Hotel Room Scene 2

When shooting a bullet to the east or west,
the **Eötvös Effect** *also affects the flight.*
When a bullet is fired in the direction of rotation of the earth,
i.e. to the east, the shots hit high. When the bullet is shot
west, the shots hit low.

—Nammo Lapua

"Curvature of the earth," announced Casey in the hotel room. Ma was napping, deep in sleep.

Johnny was reading a dime novel about Kid Lariat.

"It's called the '*Coriolis Effect*,'" continued Casey.

"This rifle shoots so far that you have to take into account the earth's curvature. Damn!

"That's why that lady's husband thought it was busted. You have to compensate, or it shoots wide."

She turned a page in the booklet.

"It gives a table of the calculations here..."

Here is the chart she copied down from the booklet:

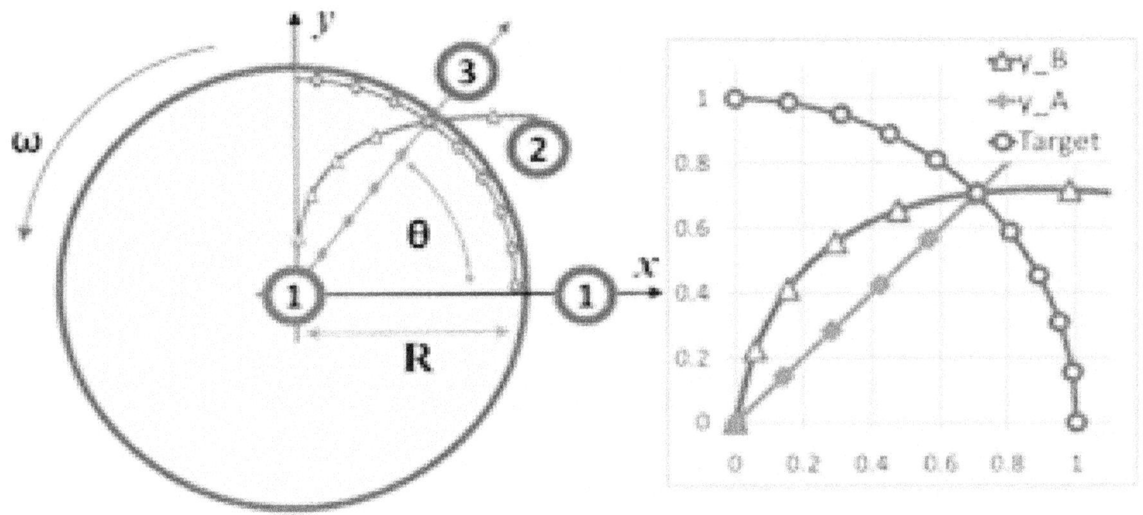

She added two columns of needed values in her notebook.

Before the Enfield rifle could be fired, she would have to compute those values, very quickly and very accurately.

A Midnight Card Game

*I don't care how you look at it,
somebody, somewhere has to take the loss.*

— ANIEDI ETUK

"Case," Moonlight tinted slightly cobalt in the street. The blue moon.

"Casey. Wake up."

Johnny's voice was stern in the darkness.

"Ma's gone."

Casey tossed on Ma's bathrobe and found a pair of slippers. Johnny cinched his gun belt.

"What time is it?" asked Casey.

"Midnight."

"Jeez. This ain't good...."

They descended the stairs to the saloon hall. Mas sat at one of the round poker tables, a drink in hand. In front of her, on the table, was a small stack of brightly colored chips and her money belt, opened.

Morgan, the militia man, had his arm half-slung around Ma's shoulders.

"There you are, kids!" she called.

"Ma, what have you — "

Casey grabbed the money belt.

"You spent our savings? Almost half is gone!"

"Don't worry, Case. I'll get it back."

"You know she can't drink," Johnny said accusingly to Angie.

"Hey!" exclaimed Casey. "That's the deed to our ranch!"

"The quit-claim," corrected Aynsley, who was reading the legal document's fine print. "Your Ma wants to use it as collateral — "

"Get your hands off her—"

Johnny shoved Morgan angrily. The militia man went sprawling. When he got up, a pistol was in his hand.

Johnny shucked and fired –

The gun flipped out of Morgan's hands. The man shouted in pain and surprise.

"I didn't even see him draw — " gasped Mrs. Aynsley.

"Hand me that deed, if you would," said Casey to the lawyer. Her voice was low and grave.

Hotel Room Scene 3 ... Rebellion

Who has written this play that we are obliged to perform?

— Eduardo Galeano

"Really?" said Casey, her features grim, her voice like steel. "You were going to bet the deed? You were willing to lose our home?"

The fury was on her.

"You can't talk to me this way!" protested Ma. "I'm your Mother!"

"Then act like it!!"

"You're not wearing the belt any more, Ma," said Case. "Deed, neither."

Ma looked helplessly from her daughter to her son.

"I'm with Case," said Johnny.

"We should have a home.," he added, to show where his thoughts lay. "We should be goin' to a school."

"You will be," said Ma. "I promise. Just one more clinic. Folsom."

Johnny, who had a soft spot for her, made no reply.

"Then straight to Albuquerque.

"I'll be good. You'll see."

Stagecoach

At 600 yards-plus, you better start crushing numbers.

— Enfield Rifle Handbook

The mountains of the Mogollon Rim stretch thirty miles across the southwest section of the New Mexico territories.

A system of high cliffs and deep canyons, brutal escarpments and dune-derived plateaus, the Mogollon Rim was created by sediments from Permian times, capped by basaltic lava flows, and given shape by glaciers, rivers and powerful winds. Cloaked in dense forests of Ponderosa Pine and Douglas Fir, the ancient mountain range lies above the Sierra Aguilada, a smaller range, and west of Gila River, in Apache lands. Their highest point is a narrow open pass often called Mimbres. Hidden in the sandstone erosion and faulting of the Mogollon Rim's vast interior are towns like Sonoma and Show Low, streams and creeks like Tonto and Yavapai, mine shafts and tribal graveyards and the Hutch Mountain Lookout.

It's one thing to read about the Mogollons, as you are now, or to see them from afar, as many do ...and it is something altogether different to be moving among them. These are wild, unpredictable spaces, haunted by ancient echoes, geographies having nothing to do with man and woman and their systems of thought. A hush emanates from the Mogollons, so they say, a somber tranquility anchored by the thousands of buried warriors of the ancient tribes, like some vast mausoleum that shares the meadows and wetlands and cloud-scudded forests with the shaggy, heavy-shouldered bison.

"These Colorado coaches," lectured the solicitor, Aynsley, "are a larger, more rugged version of the Kinnear design. Wells Fargo uses them widely.

"This is a Concorde model, if I'm not mistaken," he added. "Capacious."

Johnny glared at the talkative lawyer.

"More useless information," snorted the militia man, Morgan. He rubbed his bandaged hand sullenly.

The stagecoach's constant motion cast a bad mood within its large interior, but it was more than just the motion. The day had turned to dusk. Only an hour further to Folsom. The mountain trail was clear, the horses making good time.

"Leather-strap suspension," offered Aynsley to his captive audience, "is what gives the carriage its swinging movemen— "

It happened so fast.

All in the same moment—

They heard a thunderous crash, followed by three loud gunshots.

The horses whined their objection in a panic –

One of the brake levers snapped.

The stagecoach screeched to a halt.

The stagecoach passengers heard a hard, painful scream from the driver's seat –

"I'm hit! I'm hit!"

The stage door flew open and half of the passengers spilled falling out onto the trail –

"Shut up," came a woman's voice. A pause, and then, "Morgan! You there?"

The passengers stood. Now they could see that a great, bulky deadfall had been placed across the trail to block the stage.

Angie and Drew, from the saloon in Silver City, sat astride two horses, guns drawn.

"Hands up! All of you!" proclaimed Drew. "This here's a robbery!"

He held his pistol on the stage driver, who had his hands up. Beside him, the rifleman clutched at his arm, where had been shot.

Now Morgan smirked as he trained a gun on Johnny's stomach.

"What the devil — " sputtered Aynsley.

"You you're bandits?" demanded the startled Mrs. Aynsley.

"The money belts," commanded Morgan. "That deed! Now!"

One of the drivers groaned for mercy.

Angie stopped placing the saddle on the lead horse, turned and shot him.

"Money belts," spat Drew.

"But you're such a nice boy — "

"I'll shoot you, hey," shouted Drew, trembling.

"You'll never get away with it," warned the lawyer.

"Easy ..." said Johnny.

"Sorry, bub," Morgan said, half-smiling, to Johnny as he raised the weapon. "We can't leave witnesses now, can we?"

Ma yelled 'No!' and lunged for the militia man —

"Hey. Morgan," said Casey.

Morgan turned in time to see Casey's hand sweep to her side and emerge with a gleaming pistol, one of the Colt Rainmaker's, nickel-plated and deadly fast.

In a liquid motion, she raised the Colt and fanned the hammer —

BAMBAMBAM!

Three rounds sunk deep into Morgan's chest, all at once.

Casey swiveled and sent three more rounds slamming into anxious young Drew, jerking him clean from his saddle —

With a curse, Angie jammed her spurs into her horse and rode off —

Casey dropped the Colt and ran to grab the Enfield rifle from the passenger racks.

She shucked the rifle sheath and ran to the edge of the trail.

She stood on an outcrop facing northeast. She could see the sweep of the basin and range, to her right, where Angie was escaping —

She was galloping unseen, along the high-walled Mogollon limestone.

But there was a break in the wall, very distant ...

It was that opening to which Casey devoted her attention.

They could hear the horse's canter, moving away ...

Casey thumbed in three big, heavy cartridges.

"Eleven hundred meters ... " said Johnny.

Johnny held the rangefinder like binoculars.

He counted off a sequence of numbers.

Casey scribbled the calculations.

Distance ... curvature ... target point ... origin point

Now she watched through the Enfield's telescopic sight, following the horse-and-rider trajectory, as she imagined it.

John called out a second sequence of numbers, distance in meters.

"Twenty ..." said Johnny.

"Fifteen,,, ten .. five ..."

The Enfield let go a sharp crack —

The firearm echoed in the great solemn quiet along the southern section of the Mogollons ...

Angie's body slumped and fell from the saddle.

What we see are objects in refracted light. A thing itself does not change, just the ways in which we experience it. It is the light which changes.

A blue moon looks blue because of shifts in light, the suspended volcano dust in the air. The way that light refracts can make everything look new, and not as we thought it to be.

It alters how things appear to us, does the immense cloud of fine dust and ash from the Krakatoa Volcano, supplemented by forest fires in Sweden and Canada. When the quality of the air changes, so does the quality of light. On a Blue Moon night, the thing itself does not change, just the ways we experience it.

Casey turned to Ma.

"Why don't you take the money back to Mister Torgeson, Ma?"

She indicated the currency that had spilled from the lawyer's satchel onto the trail, when Johnny had shot Morgan.

"Back to Silver City."

Ma looked long and still at her daughter.

"I'm sure he'd appreciate it," said Casey.

She slung the Enfield over her shoulder, like it had always been there, like it belonged attached to her.

"Johnny and me can run the clinic in Folsom. Then we'll head straight for Albuquerque.

"You come join us, soon as you can."

The horses fell quiet. A silence vast and deep seemed to descend, all along the southeastern section of the Mogollon Rim. The little grouping around the stagecoach listened, as though they could all feel, or somehow hear, the rotation of the earth.

No man or woman could put an adjective to the look that appeared on Ma's face. It was sad and accepting, almost relieved and almost embarrassed, and several more emotions as well, all at the same time.

"And so the child," intoned Aynsley, "is father to the man."

"What, are you the effing chorus now?" Johnny raised his pistol to shoot the lawyer. "You two-faced *shill* — "

"No! *Please!*" Mrs. Aynsley began to cry —

"They were robbing us, too," she reminded Johnny.

Now Mrs. Aysnley's cry turned into a scream, a hideous, feral sound, for such a cultured woman —

Johnny lowered the gun. "Just as soon," he murmured.

"All right, Case," said Ma. "All good."

Ma's face had gone white. She gripped the hem of her skirt tightly

"You two ...take ..." Ma choked. "Ah! Me! Take good care, Johnny —"

"The Fort Stanton stage should be by here in an hour or so," said Casey. "That about right, Whip?" she called to the driver.

"Yup," came the reply.

Casey looked out over the basin lowlands. She closed eyes, for a moment.

"I don't know what we'll find in Albuquerque," Casey said to her brother as she swung into the saddle of the horse Drew had been riding.

"But we got a real-life deed to some damn thing.

"We got two hundred bucks."

She patted the horse's neck.

"And we can make an honest living fixin' guns."

"We should be all right," Johnny nodded.

He finished cinching the saddle of the lead stage horse and checked the horse's underbelly. The bay was ready to trade all this gunplay and confusion among the humans for an open run along a clear path.

"Let's light a shuck — "

TOM'S STORY NOTES

The mathematical theory of card counting is based on the sum of the cards that have passed, which clues us in on the cards that are left in the deck. If Reynaldo goes down with an ankle injury in minute two, the new game is different. Same here.

Card counting is possible only to the extent you can see the cards. In the case of the 'Mogollons' story, the game is casual saloon poker, in which the dealers have the habit of flipping the cards face up as they push them to the discard pile. In that moment, a card counter like Casey could see the cards that had been played, and memorize them, and calculate the new odds of the new game.

The U.S. Army hit its low point in the decades after the Civil War The western territories were too vast to patrol properly, and American had lost its taste for all things military. In my story, the Father is a gunsmith hired by individual towns and army regiments to keep their firearms in working condition. His wife and kids work in the family business. The scouts, farmers, soldiers and hunters who prowl the Great Basin and Rim would have welcomed such craftsmen.

As to snipers and the Coriolis effect ...

In this story, set in 1877, I am a little early to include a long-range rifle, but not by much. Long-range Enfields and sniper rifles started to appear on battlefields in the late 19th century, and distance snipers were common by World War I.

The actual mathematics for modern snipers is something like this:

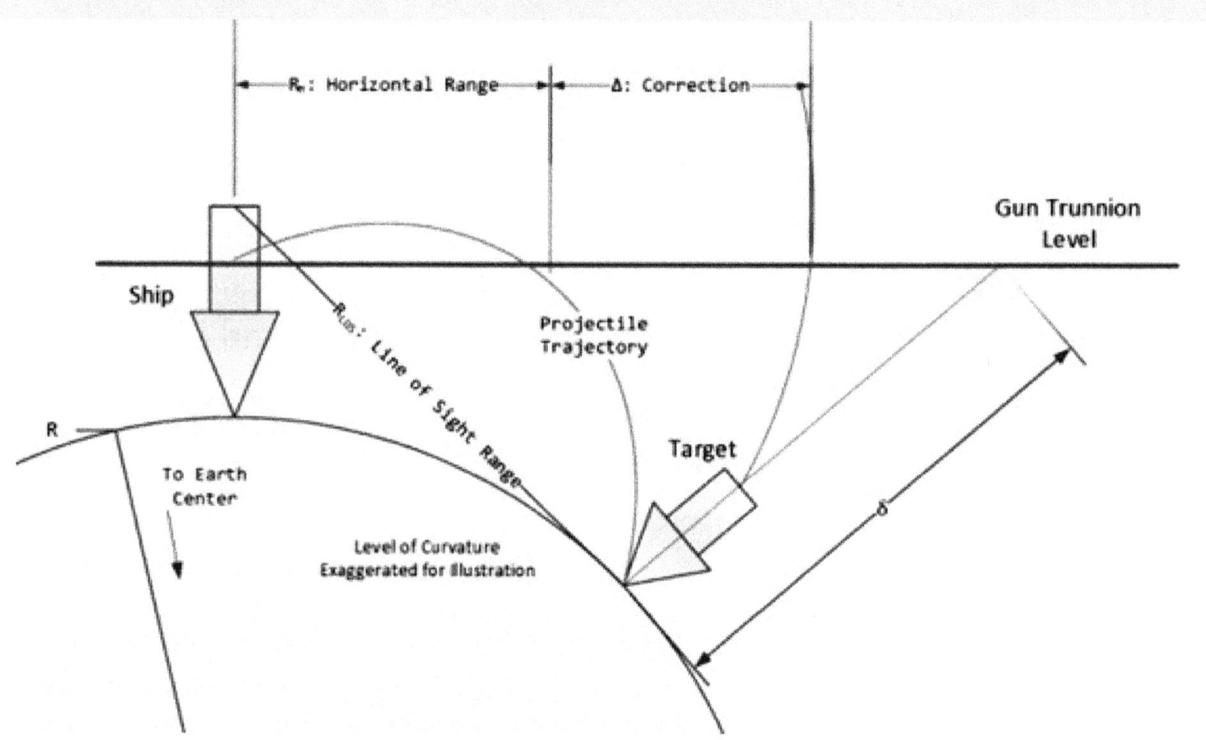

CHART OF A SAMPLE CORIOLIS EFFECT

3. Pen's Black Swan

SYNOPSIS: Penelope's school exercise turns into a bold and very specific prediction for September 16, 1992. Will a reclusive economist help her defy the markets and save her village?

A novice predicts Black Wednesday. Economic forecasting on an epic scale.

The Queen's Concern Monday, September 14, 1992

I think there's a difference between a gamble
and a calculated risk.

— EDMUND H. NORTH

The world is a bell curve.

— SIMON SINEK

"I understand we may be in for a rocky week," said the Queen. She sat on a couch in a second-story stateroom of Buckingham Palace, in central London, some seventy miles north of the falling-apart house on Lewes Lane in the village of Tifton, near Firle.

"The business with the bonds."

Over the edge of the raised teacup, her eyes watched the Finance Minister's features.

One can tell so much by close observation.

The tiny woman, Regent and Ruler, by the Grace of God, of the United Kingdom of Great Britain and Northern Ireland and of Her other Realms and Territories, Head of the Commonwealth, Defender of the Faith, thoughtfully placed her teacup back on the tray and folded her hands, waiting politely for a response.

"Quite right, your Grace," answered the Minister. "A handful of currency traders think they are very clever, and seek to take advantage by short-selling the bonds," he continued. "Only a nuisance, I assure you."

"Can we not somehow ... *block* this trading?" asked the Queen. "Outlaw it?"

> **A handful of currency traders think they are very clever. Only a nuisance, I assure you.**

It had been a most haywire year already for the Royals. No need for a crisis with the Treasury, not now, not with the Exchequer's recent resignation.

"No, I'm afraid it doesn't work that way. Now, we've done everything in our power to circumvent any type of crisis."

"Harold didn't seem to think so."

Ignoring the mention of his rival, the Finance Minister persevered. "We've approved another four billion in Pounds Sterling. We've raised the interest rates another percentage point. A number of new measures will be announced just before markets open."

"I see.

"How bad might it get?"

"The mathematics suggest," answered the Finance Minister, "that our liability is in the nine figures."

"Good God."

"This adjustment is the right thing for the Commonwealth, Majesty. In the long run," asserted the Minister. "All of your counselors agree."

The Queen looked up.

That last comment ...

All of your counselors agree was one platitude too far.

The phrase introduced a concept very different from the previous platitude of "I assure you." Now the guarantee was gone. Blame-avoidance had begun.

"And when will it all come to a head?" asked the Queen.

"Wednesday," replied the Finance Minister.

In The Kitchen Monday September 14, 1992

"Black Swan" is a metaphor for an apparent impossibility.
The term applies to an event that comes as a surprise, has a
major effect, and is often wrongly rationalized after the fact,
with the benefit of hindsight.

The term is based on an ancient belief that black swans
did not exist ... until 1697, when Dutch explorers led by Willem
de Vlamingh found a flock of black swans thriving in Western Australia.

The observation of a single black swan would be the undoing
of the logic of any system of thought.

— SALLY SCHILDHAUER, A BRIEF HISTORY OF THE NAVIGATORS

The village of Tilton, near Firle, had seen better days.

Tifton had managed well enough since the Romans. Farms raised sheep in lavender fields and managed to survive Norman invasions, royal acts of enclosure, plagues, floods and provincial dissolutions. As was true with many of the hamlets scattered among the hills and valleys of Surrey, well south of London, well north of the oceanside, Tifton endured. Barges moved up and down on the river. Birdwatchers chased though forest and pasture, sighting gadwall, coot, goldeneye, and grebes.

Then, in the early Spring of 1916, six hundred of Tifton's pride, the 10th Battalion, Royal Fusiliers, had marched off to join the European war. In

August and September of that year, Tifton's boys encountered the enemy at the upper reaches of a river called the Somme, and none returned.

The loss of an entire generation of the village' best workers was an economic blow from which the village of Tifton, near Firle, could never recover. At the Somme vanished too many off the innovators, entrepreneurs, and good managers which a thriving town needs, moving forward through changing times.

Now its picturesque cobblestone streets went unrepaired, a danger to visitors who ventured out into the English countryside from the new highways. Tree branches hung too low over the village's quaint gabled roofs. The tax base shrank. Only one of its half-dozen mills remained open, and more storefronts and pubs along High Street were shuttered every year.

This morning, in the old house on Lewes Lane, a Mother and daughter prepared for the day.

"It's not letting up, is it?"

Outside the large kitchen windows, they could see tree limbs bending and flexing in the rainstorm. The sound of water dripping into buckets served as a sort of backdrop.

"Grampa says he's coming out this morning to have another look at the roof," said the Mother. She did not sound like she believed that would help much.

Penelope, the daughter, looked at the high ceilings of the parlor and moved, step by step, to place a bucket beneath a new leak.

"Pen, were you up all night with this presentation!" said the Mother. "You actually need to sleep, you know."

"Couldn't get the arbitrage tables royt," replied Pen.

"Have you ever gone an entire actual day without saying 'actually'?" she added.

"You sound like your father more every day."

"Ozzy Ozzy Ozzy," replied Pen. "When's he coming back, anyway?"

"Next Tuesday. His flight gets in at six in the morning."

Pen snickered and took two big bites of the toast her mother had made.

"Are you chewing gum?"

"No ma'am. Toast."

Once more, she checked the triple-layered plastic wrapping around the boards for her school project. She picked them up.

She gulped a glass of orange juice.

She grabbed her yellow slicker from its hook.

"Oy! I'm off!"

"You take the bike, called the Mother.

"I'll be fine!"

"Please!"

"Actually! I can't carry the boards when I'm on the bike anyway — "

"Okay! Luck, sweetheart — "

A Car In The Rain Monday September 14, 1992

If you torture the data long enough, it will confess.

— GARY SMITH

"That poor girl — " muttered Lydia Lukashov.

Sharp-eyed Lydia Lukashov saw, through the window at her kitchen sink, through the boughs, beyond the bird-houses, the girl Penelope walking, carrying a sign or a Styrofoam board of some sort, under her slicker, through a pelting rain, down Lewes Lane.

The drenched girl was under a canopy of trees, about to walk into the unprotected pavement when the big black car drove up beside her.

"Do get in," called Lydia, minutes later, as she leaned across the front passenger seat to open the window.

She got out and helped Penelope pack the wrapped boards onto the back.

They got in the car, dripping wet.

"I was just on my way to the market," explained Lydia.

The bathrobe and slippers she wore belied that unlikely statement.

"Ta," said Pen.

"You're Penelope. Penelope West. Pen West. Your mother is the librarian, is that right? Your father is the Australian pilot. Your grandfather once ran the bank.

"I'm Lydia," she said cheerfully. "We met at the Heath Grange fundraiser.”

“Aye,’ said Pen, shaking the rainwater from her slicker. “Yer down from the unehvairsity.”

“Civil service, actually. We’re housed in Oxford, though, you’re right about that.”

Pen nodded.

The car, a clunky, antique Ford Fairlane, took the curve at the intersection awkwardly. Lydia pumped the automobile’s brakes carefully. She downshifted. They swung onto High Street

“So a pairson like you might ken a thing or tue about government,” said Penelope. “I’m guessing.”

“Yes. Certainly,” replied Lydia.

“Well. Would you consider serving as a town alderman? Alder-*woman*. It’s just that my Grandad is acting Mayor. And he’s getting on a bit. We haven’t a clue, really.”

They took the High Street fork. The school was to the left, the market to the right.

“Yes,” answered Lydia Lukashov. “I will consider it, Pen West.”

The Ford Fairlane arrived at the high school.

“Here we are. Take my umbrella, won’t you? I have too many — ”

“Yo’re very kind, ma’am.”

The car door closed.

Penelope trotted into the school, boards tucked under her arm.

The Math Classroom Monday September 14, 1992

Measure twice. Cut once.

— Carpenters' motto

"Very good. Very good," said the Instructor, Mr. Preshaw, to the Advanced Mathematics class, twenty minutes later. "Very exciting."

"All right. What are we doing today? Melissa Quarles, what are we doing?

"Something something risk," replied Melissa.

"Almost. We are looking into *practical applications of mathematics* in particular the measurement of risk.

"As you will recall, Miss Quarles here challenged the class, challenged me, and asked *What good is algebra?*' What's the point of studying Calculus, or Statistics, or Geometry?

"The answer is this: market forces."

"Understand them or suffer. It is market forces which have taken our village to the brink. And it is market forces – and your understanding of them – which can bring it back.

"Critical thinking!" he urged.

"This morning, we are pleased that two of our students have taken up the challenge.

"Presentation One. Risk and Sports Forecasting. Robbie Meaks. Let's give him a hand."

Cheers rose, mixing with jeers when the student propped a board on the easel to reveal the famous Premier league blue-and-yellow crest. Alongside it was a photo of striker Lee Chapman scoring against Man United. Here is the formula that began sports-outcome probabilities:

$$P(A \mid B) = P(B \mid A) \bullet P(A) / P(B)$$

Twenty-five minutes and many questions later, Robbie Meaks sat down, to applause.

"Outstanding. Outstanding." Mr. Preshaw stood. "That is some critical thinking!

"Remember: in sports, or in investments, the smaller the standard deviation of results, the more consistent the performance is, and therefore the easier to predict.

"Now." He rubbed his hands together. "For our second presentation. Miss Penelope West." A new round of cheers went up – mostly *Ozzie Ozzie Ozzie* — for Pen was well-liked.

She rose, removing the gum from her mouth.

"Calculating risk in the financial markets," said Mr. Preshaw. "This one is quite something. Wake up, Hanson."

"Through her forecasting, our Penelope believes she has uncovered an anomaly. A rare event."

Here was her first slide:

Threat x Vulnerability x Cost = Risk

"Now, let's give each of these a value." Penelope walked to the chalkboard.

"Values based on current events regarding the British pound sterling ..."

.9 times Zero times 1K = Zero

She re-wrote the equation on the blackboard, this time with numbers for Threat, Vulnerability. Cost and Risk.

"But you've got the risk at zero," Robbie pointed out. "There is no such thing."

The class grew quiet.

"Zero risk," asserted Pen.

"Black Swan," smiled Mr. Preshaw. "Pen thinks we have may ourselves a black swan."

Penelope opened the presentation boards.

Visit To Harold, Tuesday September 15, 1992

*No formula in finance tells you that
the moat is 28 feet wide and 16 feet deep.*

— WARREN BUFFETT

At 4:00 p.m. sharp, that same day, the doorbell rang in the big house uphill from Lewes Lane.

"You've dressed up," commented the tall man. "You shouldn't have — "

Harold Heidigger, leading economist of the Western World, lately Chancellor of the Exchequer, opened the door. A tall, sour man, Heidigger had a bristly aspect dominated by bushy eyebrows above a beak-like nose.

In the doorway stood a teenaged girl.

She was chewing gum. She wore two layers of frayed plaid shirts, a school skirt, socks rolled down to the ankles, and tennis sneakers. A cascade of unruly hair was being unsuccessfully restrained by two red barrettes.

"You should talk," replied Penelope.

Harold Heidigger wore dark corduroy slacks and a frayed cardigan, the uniform of genteel poverty among eminent professors.

"Quite the tosser, you ahh."

Harold Heidigger laughed.

"He started it, Miss."

"I know. He's very full of himself.

"Do come in, Penelope. You've dried out!

"Hello, Mister Preshaw, I'm Lydia. We spoke on the phone. How are you?"

"Very well, Miss Lukashov. Thanks for seeing us on such short notice."

"A pleasure. This is Harold. My very rude husband — "

Wednesday September 16, 1992

*In Britain, Black Wednesday, which occurred on
September 16, 1992, is now known as the day when speculators
"broke the pound." This euphemism is used to describe
the moment in time when market forces coalesced
to force the British government to exit the European Exchange Rate
Mechanism by removing its currency from that agreement.*

— KATRINA MUNICHIELLO

An office phone rang.

The sound echoed softly in the sleek spaces of the modern spaces of the 34th floor of One Canada Square, latest addition to the row of Canary Wharf skyscrapers.

"Let's hold the calls, shall we?" requested the public relations woman in her satin voice.

"The Minister's here — "

She escorted the Finance Minister and his two associates down three steps and into her firm's reception room. Soft light reflected off chrome-accented furniture. The lively, friendly melody and upbeat rhythms of Dave Brubeck's Take Five album floated in the air.

The pair mixed easily among the slick-haired traders, staffers, and financiers in red suspenders, bow ties, and pinstriped suits, among the slim female forms in pastel dresses.

The offices of the Finance Ministry had been closed for the day.

The observation of a single black swan would be the undoing of the logic of any system of thought.

The Finance Minister pulled a greenish-gray Nokia 101 cell phone from his jacket pocket. He glanced at the small green screen. He turned the device off.

Wine glasses in hand, people had gathered on a large Oriental carpet, a large Bokhara rug, of saturated reds and blue-gold borders, to watch a large-screen television mounted on a wall.

BBC REPORTER
It's quite a scene here, Marsha. Unprecedented.
It's a trading frenzy, with all the trading going in one direction: from the
British Treasury into a single trader's bank account.
Since the departure from the Euro was announced,
a scenario like this has been considered possible but remote ...

Two more office phones rang.

"Leslie!" barked the PR woman. "Turn all phones off, won't you?

BBC REPORTER
I don't know if you can hear me over the cacophony,
but basically the Finance Ministry's bluff has been called.
By the former Exchequer, Harold Heidigger.

He has mounted a brazen attack on the British pound.
As viewers may recall, Heidigger's departure three months
ago was a bitter one …

Waiters carrying trays of rose wine glasses and napkin-wrapped
appetizers stopped to watch events unfold on the television screen.

BBC ANCHOR
Yes, we can see the devaluation pick up speed,
even as we speak. Martin, what is being done
to mitigate what appears to be a very bleak day
indeed, for the Crown —

BBC REPORTER
Not a thing. This appears to be a risk-free bet
for Heidigger. The only silver lining here may be
the rumor that Heidigger is turning all his
proceeds over to a non-profit —

BBC ANCHOR
All right! Now we go to our analysts,
standing by in studio and in
the offices of Deutsche Bank —

Now came the sound of heels clicking on marble floor.

The Secretary trotted unceremoniously into the reception area, wielding a cell phone —

"Leslie! What on earth — "

"It's the Queen, Ma'am!" said Leslie.

"For the Finance Minister."

The concern in Leslie's voice and in her posture was unmistakable.

"Calling from the Palace.

"The Prime Minister is with her ..."

Aftermath Sunday September 27, 1992

*If you hear a "prominent" economist using the word
"equilibrium" or "normal distribution," do not argue with him;
just ignore him, or try to put a rat down his shirt.*

— Nassim Nicholas Taleb,
The Black Swan: The Impact of the Highly Improbable

The flock of saw-winged swallows came across the lavender fields at a shallow angle, searching for a particular row of outdoor feeders near the Library-and-Town Hall complex in the village of Tifton, near Firle.

They passed over a village busy with new activities unseen by the birds before now. The friendly sounds of hammering and calls among the workers and supervisors rose, as did the sounds of cement trucks and the steam of asphalt where roads were being repaired. They heard church bells and beeping as the mason trucks backed up to contribute to the new construction. Ladders and panes of glass marked new storefronts appearing along High Street. Surveyors measured for a widening of Lewes Lane.

And everywhere were roofers, clambering in their kneepads, laying new tiles and tar to keep the rains out.

"Will the meeting come to order."

The new Mayor smacked the gavel sharply.

She looked at the room full of her village friends with an air of friendly command, encouraging and challenging at the same time, like a volleyball coach.

The entire population of Tifton, near Firle, was in attendance. The buzz in the room abated slowly.

"All right!" said Penelope.

Close behind her sat her Mother, Grandfather, and two of Grampa's old banker colleagues, smiling town elders.

Beside the young new Mayor sat Mr. Preshaw on one side, and Lydia Lukashov on the other.

Rolls of architectural plans and city maps lay on the tables.

"Lit's git stahted," said Pen. "We've got a lot to go ovah … "

TOM'S STORY NOTES

Black Wednesday actually happened, and on the date used in my story.

A currency trader named George Soros realized at some point during the previous week that the British Treasury had no options. They had made the mistake of announcing their decision to remove the British pound from the European Exchange. Once announced, this was a decision they could not change. Seeing this, Soros stacked up a bet of more than a billion dollars shorting the pound – that is, gambling the currency's value would have to fall. He bet correctly.

In this story, Pen could only have made such a 'black swan' forecast with the benefit of a huge tipoff – from her grandfather, the village banker. Once he pointed out to Pen that the Finance Ministry had painted itself into a corner, she could then demonstrate through her forecasting what the outcomes of the Crown's decision might be.

Pen and her father, the pilot, appear in the forthcoming Aviation collection.

In terms of your personal finances, here is one of the most important lessons I have for each of my classes:

If I place a penny on a chessboard square, and then place two pennies on the next square, and then 4 on the next and then 8 on the next and then keep doubling the amount until the chessboard is full, how much money will I have?

    a)   *680 dollars*

    b)   *11,200 dollars*

    c)   *18 trillion dollars*

The answer, of course, is 18 trillion dollars.

This is a retelling of the semi-famous 'wheat and chessboard' story and it is actually a lesson in the power of compounding. Sometimes called 'geometric progression.'

Ignore the power of geometric progression at your financial peril.

Two extremely important words for you: Roth IRA.

4. Jayani's Big Gamble

Synopsis: Third Aunt, who raised young apprentice baker Jayani as her own child, is gravely ill. Now Jayani must somehow raise seventy gold shivasi for the trek to the Vedic doctors in the next province. A traveler suggests a most unusual way to do so.

Jayani will need all her skills with the abacus – and learn new ones – if she is to save Third Aunt from an excruciating death.

Prologue: An Urgent Need

From the eastern sea to the western sea, the area
in between the Himalayas and the Vindhyas,
is what wise men call the land of the Aryans ...
beyond it is the country of the barbarians.

– Manusmriti, Second Century B.C. Book of Law

Now Third Aunt was coughing blood.

The healers, despite all their ministrations, gave up.

"A better world awaits her," said Chikistak, one of the healers. "And soon."

Third Aunt squeezed Jayani's hand with her own.

She eventually stopped coughing.

The old woman slept, but fitfully. Her breath was labored. Her bent spine kept her in a curved position.

"What if I can get her to the clinic in Pataliputra," asked Jayani. "The Vedic doctors ..."

"Yes. They might fix this. But it costs money," said Chikistak.

"Do you have it?"

"How much is it?" asked Jayani.

He told her.

The girl shook her head. The blood had drained from her face.

The coughing started up again.

It was getting worse.

"I am strong, sister," said Ganesh, when the healers had gone. "I can work harder! In the next rotation, I might be a wagon-boy."

"You're eight," Jayani told her little brother.

Later, deep in the night, hidden among the murmurs of the night prayers and rustlings among the camels, the boy could see the silhouette of his sister out on the sands, alone, and he could hear the forlorn sound of her crying.

Morning At The Ovens

The power of pure thought has shaped
our world for over two millenia.

— JIM AL-KAHLILI

"You are Jayani," said the tall traveler the next morning. "The Oven-Master's apprentice."

The Arab cast a shadow as he stood in the courtyard of the kilns compound. He was cloaked in black. A servant knelt behind him. His speaking voice was rich with influences, syllables and vowels and cadences from other lands.

"Aye, *yaatree*," answered the oasis girl, turning to face the visitor. She might have used the term *musafirin*, but she was not yet sure about him.

"I am Jayani."

This fateful exchange took place in the age of the Mughal princes, self-involved Mirza Abu Bakr and the ever-incompetent Rafi-ush-Shan, at an oasis named Ahichhatra, which lay some small distance from the northern highway known as Uttarapatha, in the Valley of the Gangee.

The watering-hole community nestled in the dusty lower hills of the Gongotri was a beehive of activities.

Jayani stood in front of the second cylindrical oven, holding an oversized kiln paddle, in her gloved hands.

As slight a figure as the stranger was imposing, the girl Jayani, only fourteen, stood straight and calm, even when the Arab stepped closer.

"I am Salim Abdallah al-Ayyashi."

He signaled to his servant.

"I come lately from the Christian lands. Bound for Changsha."

The girl squinted in the morning sunlight.

"Won't you bake this for me," said the traveler evenly.

The Arab's servant unwrapped a large platter and handed it to Jayani.

"It would be a great favor."

Jayani, hard-working apprentice of the communal ovens, removed the big leather gloves from her hands. She stuck them in the pocket of the blue apron she wore.

It was a Govindan *upahaar*, a ceramic platter, one of a kind.

Its ivory surface showed the outlines of carvings. Looking closely, you could see circular patterns figures, the delicate   articulation of some vision. Those hidden painted patterns would emerge, turning into vibrant colors if the platter was properly glazed, at the correct heat, for the correct length of time.

"This is the work of Nabil Matar," said Jayani.

The Arab nodded. "A heavenly scene. A gift for Yikuang, the Manchu prince.

"His wife has given birth to a son."

Jayani handed it back.

"It is a most elegant thing," said the girl. "Rare. And I will not be the clod who ruins it."

"Ibn Batuta recommends you," said the Arab. "He speaks of you as an artist."

"The Moroccan is too generous with his praise."

Zrimat, Ovens-Master, hovered nearby, sensing an exchange of coins.

"Of course," Salim Abdallah al-Ayyashi challenged Jayani. "If you think you are incapable of such a task …"

Jayani turned to face the bank of ovens nestled into the rock. She saw the impossible jumble of generations of clever bakers and smelters applying all manners of flame and heat to all manners of substances. Here stood Venetian vertical stoves, four active half-cylinder ovens which dominated the commerce, with wooden pallets hung alongside. And there were deck ovens as well, and behind them, squat, square Vulcans and clay chamber stoves, clusters of dwarf cob (mud, that is) furnaces. Along the sides of the bake-shop lay open char pits lined with coals, half-buried wood-fired roasters, columns of pottery kilns. There were dusty banks of *fourneau*, or chimneyed bread ovens. Two kang platform stoves towered over the left batteries. There were kilns for pottery, some abandoned, and blazing furnaces for metal. She saw cauldron-hung fire-pits for stews and open roasters for poultry. Spits for large fish. Earthen kilns for dye and a section of domed beehive ovens, or skep, such as the long-dead butchers and bakers and culinaries used when they prepared the wedding feasts of Qasim Abdallah.

"Come back after lunch," Jayani told Salim Abdallah al-Ayyashi.

Every particle, every brushstroke, every atom of the ceramic platter's latent beauty had come to life.

"This is … fine work. Very fine. It is beyond my hopes," breathed Salim

Abdallah al-Ayyashi.

The purples and ruby reds and midnight-blue hues on the plate had emerged in lacquered glory, and the more somber ochres and ambers as well. The Arab traveler swore that Matar himself would blush to see it. One could now see the carving's influences – Persian, Indian, even European. Winged figures carrying birds which had been invisible before were now prominent, and the symbols would please and mystify those of the Middle Kingdoms for years to come. One of the shepherds invented a song about the platter, its fine glaze, and the iron-rich clays, and the brave young oven-keep who had brought the pigments to life.

A crowd gathered spontaneously.

He held the piece aloft.

"All the Mughal lands will hear of this!"

The Ovens-Master, Zrimat, inserted himself.

"It took my assistant three hours' labor," the Ovens-Master reminded the Arab. "Plus customized details ... "

Salim Abdallah al-Ayyashi smiled and paid with a flourish that implied it would have been cheap at ten times the price.

Zrimat rolled the coins along his fingers. He counted them twice. He placed the bag of coins in his jacket pocket. None did he pass on to his apprentice, Jayani.

A Pre-Dawn Visit

We just had the discussion.

—BRIAN BURNS

Very late that same night, so late it was almost morning, a tall figure appeared in the entrance to the hut which was home to Third Aunt, the girl Jayani and her brother, Ganesh.

Only the camels stirred, milling among the spring fountains and banked fires.

Jayani rubbed her eyes to see the Arab trader Salim Abdallah al-Ayyashi in her home.

"We depart for points East," murmured he. "We offer our thanks."

He placed a heavy bag on the dining table.

"Fruits. For pajee. Scorbutus."

A second heavy bag. "You already have a touch of it, too, by the look."

Now he placed a third bag, lighter than the first two.

"Herbs. For rickets. Calcium, to lengthen the bones. For her." He nodded to sleeping figure of Third Aunt.

"Plant the stems on a northern slope."

"Mashallah," said Jayani, and Salim Abdallah al-Ayyashi smiled to hear this, a correction of her previous remark. "Allah has willed it."

She bowed low and sincerely, for this was no idle token.

"A Frenchman named Bernier will be passing this way. I will send him word. He will have more for you."

"My thanks, Prince among Travelers."

"God wills it." The Arab smiled.

"One last thing, Jayani.

"Those old ovens are your oasis' treasure. If you can restore them, all the tribes of the Northern Valleys will seek you out.

"Those main ovens, with shelving, could hold twice as much meat. And ceramics in all the small ones. You can do the delicate work as well as the volume work. Higher margin."

"To what end?" asked Jayani. "Zrimat keeps it all."

"It doesn't have to be that way." He explained his idea. He said it works well in among the Ottomans, and in the larger villages, those with Western ways.

Those old ovens are your oasis' treasure. If you can restore them, all the tribes of the Northern Valleys will seek you out.

"You can charge well for such work. More than enough to take your Aunt to the Vedic doctors.

"But first you need to calibrate the volumes. Those volumes interior to each separate oven. With accuracy. If you lose control over the volumes, if the heat becomes uneven ... "

"But how can I measure those spaces?" Jayani asked. "They are irregular."

"They are varied," corrected the Arab. "Each has a dimension that can be calculated and recorded. The contours follow specific shapes.

"You'll see." He took out paper from a satchel the servant carried. He drew on it.

Here is what he drew:

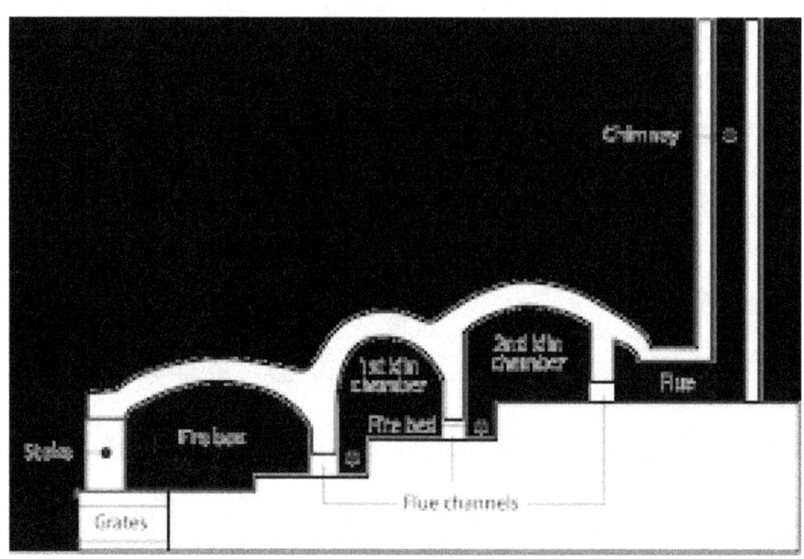

A Proposal

"Did you say you wish to rent the ovens?" asked the Council Chief, Ajmal.

Ajmal did not sound angry, or surprised, she sounded like she wanted clarity. Ajmal was a stout woman, tall, solid, big-shouldered and sharp-eyed.

"At *night?*"asked another of the Council. "Is that what you said?"

"Yes, Elder," said Jayani. "I propose to rent the ovens each night. For a fortnight."

"What hours?" asked Amjal.

"Midnight to dawn," replied the girl.

It had been three months since the tall Arab traveler's comments.

The evening sun was low on the horizon. The Council fire burnt steadily.

"What price can you offer, dear?" asked Ajmal.

"Five hens. Two roosters. And two bushels of rice."

"So much?" asked the stablemaster.

"How can such a thing be?" demanded another. "Your Aunt is a stables-sweeper ..."

"My family and I have saved for this," Jayani asserted. "We were saving to take Third Aunt to Pataliputra."

"And now you want to rent the ovens instead?"

"I know those ovens," continued the girl, "and my proposal is an honorable one. Well this serves the *qabila*," she declared.

She was smart to use this phrase, much beloved among the Ahichhatra, a phrase that might translate today to 'the common good.'"

Hands akimbo, Jayani spoke no further.

The slender figure stood, silhouetted against the full moon.

Along the perimeter, near the watchtowers, a pair of donkeys brayed in some nocturnal episode among the livestock. Was that a camel, snickering?

"Such an arrangement is without precedent," protested Zrimat.

"Besides, the ovens need to recover at night. The ... the mortar can become fatigued. It is well-known that the clay and mortar ... can become *fallow* — "

"No it isn't!" called the terraced-slope farmers, who despised Zrimat.

"You just made that up!"

There followed a lively discussion.

Jayani was asked to wait by the ovens.

The Council voted.

She was called back.

"The Council grants your request, young lady," said Amjal. "Starting Saturday. The payment is due Friday noon.

"We ask that you donate half the profits of this enterprise, if it is such. To the village. It will go toward building a barn for the camels."

The fire crackled.

"Agreed," replied Jayani.

Experiments With The Various Kilns: Volumes Of A Tandoor

Mathematics, for all its abstractions,
is a communal and human activity.

— Eugenia Chang

"Do you mean *tasbih?*" asked Saraya, the seamstress, coming down sharply on that last word, for that would have meant something.

"No. Not *tasbih,*" replied Jayani. She had not brought the topic up in the first place, and cared not to explain it, not to show how much she knew.

"Like *tasbih,* but not the same."

Jayani stoked one of a small bank of the clay ovens.

She shut the chamber doors. She deftly checked the temperature at either end, and on the top and bottom. She made careful notations.

"Then what?" asked the woman. "This divination must come from somewhere — "

"Geometry," said Jayani.

"And is that the Arabic system? Is it that which the Pharaohs used...?"

Jayani nodded that it was, indeed.

"Ah!" said Saraya. She nodded, satisfied.

"Those missing shelves," said the mason, a Samanid man as thin as a shadow. He had stopped on his way from the quarries, and rested his brimming wheel-barrow, to regard the oven banks. He had not spoken for some time.

"They're for cakes."

This remark changed everything.

"Here."

He pointed a long index finger.

He pointed to the rusted, dust-covered hinges along the upper walls on either side of the open furnace, and the long metal supports, unused for many years.

Dark-eyed Jayani knew exactly where he was looking.

She carefully closed the stove doors and opened them again.

Jayani had long imagined an upper section to the much-used meat kilns, a sort of internal balcony. Such an addition to the ovens' capacity would dramatically increase their output.

But it could not be regulated …

"I saw the furnaces at Sunak," continued the mason. "There, the bakers shunted the excess heat of the big stacks in ways so as to fire the confection ovens. Like overflow. Like a dam.

"It is well considered, artisan," said the mason to Jayani as he bent and raised his wheelbarrow. "You will solve the problem, of that I am sure.

"May the coral-crowned Queens of Khurasan guide you."

Jayani was already drawing a new configuration based on his suggestion, and only managed to shout her thanks when he was almost out of sight.

He heard, and waved.

A fully-grown camel weighs 1300 pounds.

A camel can drink two hundred liters of water in three minutes.

A camel has a third, transparent eyelid that serves to dislodge dust from its eyes.

Most livestock lose 20 to 40 liters per day. Camels lose a mere 1.3 liters of fluids every day.

That evening, Jayani and Third Aunt and the mother camel watched as the calf Al-Layth ibn Al-Saffar attempted to lie down for her rest.

Tentatively, the beast bent one knee. After several tries, she managed to get a front knee solidly planted. She quickly followed it with a second knee.

Then the back legs lowered, and her full weight fell. Finally, the calf rested her neck and head on the ground, legs folded neatly under the torso.

Huh.

Everything in its place, thought Jayani.

Just so ...

"See this?" Jayani asked Ganesh.

She held up a door of a cylindrical stove.

It had taken three days to disassemble and clean and reassemble the various ovens in the wall of kilns. Jayani had paid two of the young shepherds to help.

"We have to find out how much it holds."

"Can't we just look at it and tell?" asked little brother.

"No. We can't just guess. We need to know for sure. To know exactly.

"So all we do is measure the width, the length, and the height.

"Now multiply these three."

Volume.

"And when we have an irregular shape within the box, we simply subtract its volume ... like so."

Ganesh nodded, satisfied at the process.

"What do you mean 'multiply'?" he asked, after a minute.

Several times, when Ganesh and Third Aunt were asleep, Jayani explained her tables to the camel calf, Al-Layth ibn Al-Saffar.

Al-Layth ibn Al-Saffar was well pleased, nodding and chewing as the girl spoke, letting the stream of murmured words splash over her.

The camel calf seemed to favor simple addition and subtraction, and tended to ignore anything to do with multiplication or geometry. She tried to spit on the tablet and abacus whenever Jayani brought up triangles.

Calculating Kiln Volume

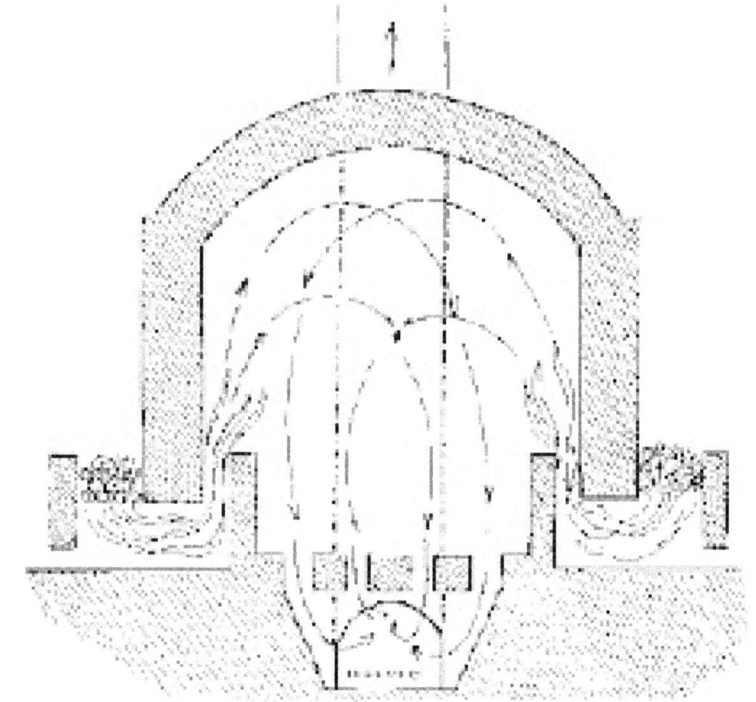

1.   Volume of a sprung arch kiln: Volume = Width x Depth x (height of the side wall + 2/3 of the rise)

2.   Volume of a catenary kiln: Volume = Depth x Arch Area (4/3 height x 1/2 base width)

Late that evening, one of the camels, a popular female named Eshanamaaz brayed, asking to be let out, back into the pastures, to graze some more.

"Because you're so special, is that it?" called Jayani.

The air was rich with odors of meats stewing at a low flame, stewing overnight, and smoke from the fires in the lookout towers.

"Request denied. Go to sleep."

Conclusion: A Month Later

These things tend to escalate.

— Julian Broudy

Word spread.

Travelers along the northern highway of Uttarapatha took a growing interest in the girl Jayani and her ovens. The bold gamble she had taken intrigued pilgrims and camel-drivers always eager for a good story. All manner of the curious crowded the *tandoor*, the communal ovens of the oasis called Ahichhatra.

The onlookers took pleasure when a Turkish tea set emerged from one of the European stoves in a molten lump. *Such a thing!*

They inquired respectfully about the mathematics, and the designs and distinctions and capacities among the many ovens and kilns, until Jayani took to locking the gate to the tandoor compound.

Jewelry emerged from the kilns of Ahichhatra, running day and night, and slabs of mutton, roasted grain, smelted silver, and more.

Her constant experimentations with charts and volume and equations gave rise to improvement, moving things here and there, making adjustments, each noted by the onlookers. She developed a team of boy porters, to carry merchandise to and from the ovens down the foot paths to the Bakhari Road, with its many caravans and wagons and travelers.

An elderly apothecary came to her with minutely detailed instructions for simmering certain custom-brewed medicines. A family of toolmakers came over the Sijara with curved blades for swords.

So many customers.

Official agents of the Achaemenid asked her to mint a batch of the gold quarter *svana* coins, and the small, square bronze purana, as well as die-struck *saurashta* , the face of which caused some uproar among the Gandhara veterans.

The Frenchman, Bernier, arrived three months later. One of the items he brought, as gifts from Salim Abdallah al-Ayyashi, was a small, intricate Venetian metal-wrapped-in-cloth device that measured temperature. A second gift was dried fish, for Third Aunt's condition. While he himself was churlish, and arrogant, Bernier delivered a helpful set of suggestions regarding cooling the cylindrical ovens.

"We forgot to calculate the differences in slope," concluded Jayani one afternoon. This realization was followed by a string of oaths.

Only the camel calf they had named Al-Layth ibn Al-Saffar, who had taken to following Jayani everywhere, was there to hear.

"It is a mistake we can correct, loyal one," Jayani told her, once she had calmed down.

If she had been worried, the young camel gave no sign of it, but continued to work her jaws unevenly on a wad of grass as she stood patiently, nearby the girl Jayani.

Jayani sent for one of the younger Vedic doctors, to ride from Pataliputra. He stayed for days, tending Third Aunt. He charged much for the visit.

Third Aunt began to heal.

The fruits and herbs took hold. The Vedic doctor showed Chikistak how to harvest the berries, and to make poultices from the juices.

Plantings were made all along the northern slopes.

The Council made the night-time oven-rental contract permanent, over Zrimat's objections.

When the new rotations were announced, Jayani had been rotated two stations higher, to Master Baker.

Zrimat was rotated to Assistant Sweeper of the Stables.

Third Aunt slept in a cushioned bed, in a house with four rooms.

Jayani rubbed lotion on her hands and spent time tending the camels whenever she could, calling them each by name, chastising them for their wickedness, enjoying their dark humor.

And each night, the recumbent camels slept smiling beneath a platter of stars, dreaming of coral-crowned queens in blue oceans.

TOM'S NOTES

A smart entrepreneur named Ross Perot did this same thing with IBM in Houston, Texas in the 1960's. Realizing the great potential of the bank of computers which complacent IBM used 9 to 5, Perot rented out their machines overnight and put their calculating potential to a different and fuller usage.

In this story, Jayani is simply measuring the outside of each kiln – whether it is cylindrical or rectangular — then calculating its volume. The she figures the thickness of the walls and irregular shapes – arches, curved walls – inside the oven and subtracts those volumes from the master shell volume.

In a region where Arabic and Hindu influences mix, I have tried to use some subtlety when to comes to language and names. At the end, Salim smiles when Jayani uses an Arab blessing rather than Hindi, as she had done when they first met. A show of respect.

This story came quickly, once I realized that I needed something clear, fun (with a satisfying reversal) and short. The goal is to lure readers into the deep waters of stories like 'The Architect' and 'The Case of the Shy Mathematician' and the upcoming Aleutians epic.

A sub-theme in this story is caste. Had I written it differently, or if I were to rewrite it today, it might have figured more prominently.

The real problem I had in writing this story was to keep it short. I had to continually cut back, and prevent myself from filling out the details of historical context, tribal rivalries underlying, technical systems, coinage, and other BS that mostly serves to irritate readers. I have tried to keep the stories almost abstract, free of clutter, running along only those axes that propel the dilemma and the reversal. There is an entire dimension of heat measurement which I avoided.

As with several of the adventures, I found things veering off into engineering, when all I mean to spotlight is the math.

5. Sasha with the Red Hair

SYNOPSIS: Uly takes the train to Moscow to collect an award for her work in Derivations, but as usual, her beautiful, red-headed sister Sasha steals all of the attention. When the family arrives to stay with a professor cousin, Uly becomes entranced with the Maya tablet the professor (Yuri Knosorov) is studying. The ensuing code-breaking triggers unexpected events.

A wicked sister gets what she deserves. A young mathematician unlocks an ancient mystery

The Train To Moscow

"You're a *bad* parent!" Sasha informed her poor father. She brushed her mane of spectacular red hair as she spoke, as was the vain girl's habit.

"And if anyone ever wrote a TEXTBOOK on how to be a bad parent," continued Sasha, "you would be IN it! You'd be FEATURED, actually. Except that you couldn't even READ it!"

Sasha, the favored child, could get away with this kind of talk.

"Have some kielbasa," replied Father. "You're tired and hungry, is all."

"Only if I can have some WINE with it — " pouted Sasha with the Red Hair.

"I told you, Sasha. You're only 16. Girls your age don't drink. We're not French, after all — "

The train car leaned a bit too far to the left as it navigated a turn.

The disgruntled Proskouriakoff family from the black-earth region, Russian's rich farmland. was spread out on opposing seats of the once-elegant, bamboo- woven cushions of the Moscow-bound train.

Riding the trains from the Southern Provinces was always an

adventure, in the Winter of 1957 as it no doubt it still today. The locomotive stopped in Tambov Oblast, then again at Pavelestsky Station, passengers disembarking for the gauge switch.

Two different railway gauges in the same nation – can you imagine?

Only in Russia.

"I'm going to the food car, then to see the engines," announced Uly, standing. "I'm taking Lev with me."

She was the younger, smarter, less glamorous of the two Proskouriakoff girls. Sasha with the Red Hair began to mount an objection to Uly's proposed expedition, but Father spoke first.

"You'll get no money from me," said Father coldly. "This trip is already costing me a small fortune."

"I have my own money," replied Uly.

"And the prize that I won brings four hundred rubles." Which he knew.

"Huh! Big shot."

Father wrung his hands, rattled by his daughter's independence.

"So much like your mother …"

A farmer, the strict task-master of eighty collective-owned acres of black-earth soil and a dozen head of cattle, Father Proskouriakoff was out of his element on this train to the big city.

Uly took the hand of her little brother, Lev.

She and Lev walked down the rolling train aisle.

"We'll be back soon," she said.

Every child's relationship to their parents is different.

"Tickets," called the Conductor. "Tickets, please."

"Is that an award? An honor of some sort?" asked the kindly woman in the seat across from theirs, once the Conductor had passed.

The lady leaned over to inspect the silver medal with the sun corona and a long red ribbon. It lay on the seat next to Sasha.

"Yes," answered Father. "My daughter won the Vavilov. It's a Math Prize.

"We're going to Moscow for my certificate ceremony," added Sasha.

"That sounds important," smiled the lady. "What kind of mathematics?"

"Celestial Physics," replied Sasha proudly. "The celestial physics of African monkeys. It's very important work."

"Sasha," Father chuckled, for it was Uly who had won the prize.

"Well!" exclaimed the lady in the next seat. "You must be very smart."

"Yes, I am!" nodded Sasha. "I am tired from all my mathematical efforts! But your kind words are a balm, Madame."

Father smirked.

Sasha was so funny.

"You have friends in Moscow?" asked the nice lady.

"In Moezey Moskvi. We are staying with my wife's cousin," replied Father. "She's the wife of the linguist, Knorozov."

The train whistled, warning sheep and carts and curious creatures to stay away from the tracks.

Then the lady in the next seat leaned close, as if to inspect the medal and ribbon.

"A word to the wise," said she to Father in a low, confidential voice.

"Best not to attract attention. One never knows who is listening, these days."

The lady patted Sasha

"What lovely hair."

She straightened Sasha's scarf, as thoughtful women will do for the young.

As she did, she dropped a very small – no larger than a thimble – electronic listening device into Sasha's bag.

In A Moezey Moskvi Apartment

If Greek civilization explored the universe
with geometry, the Maya did so with arithmetic and time.

— TIME AMONG THE MAYA

Father knocked on the door.

He knocked again.

The four members of the black-earth branch of the Prouskieff family huddled in the cold hallway on the sixth-floor apartment. The Moezey Moskvi neighborhood of Moscow was home to the Moscow State Linguistic University.

The scowling linguist, Yuri Knorozov, whipped open the door.

"Are you the plumber?" he asked Father, scowling.

Not waiting for the answer, Knorozov disappeared from the doorway.

"I thought you said two cycles above the *alautun*," said a voice from around the corner sternly, almost shouting.

Knorozov's wife, Yanina, came to the door. She was a guarded, elegant woman, from one of the eastern tribes.

"You're Bella's husband," she stated.

"You've come at a bad time."

"Yet," Father reminded her, "you seemed to enjoy the timing of our truck when we brought potatoes last Spring. During the famine."

Farming is hard, comprehensively hard, a most grueling calling, nearly impossible to do well, hard in a thousand ways, in ways only those who war daily with nature can understand.

Not much scares a farmer.

Father was not going anywhere.

"Come in," said Yanina.

The rambling apartment in Moezey Moskovi was spacious, run-down, and filled with drab furniture, cigarette smoke and Maya representations.

For Moscow, the musty flat was almost palatial. Chandeliers from Stalin's era set off the high-ceilinged main parlor. Once-fashionable mauve drapes hung at the windows. An entire wall of bookshelves bent the wooden floors slightly.

Human murmuring and arguing came through a double doorway that led to a study. Scholarly work had spilled from the study out into the high-ceilinged main parlor, where small desks, desk chairs, lamps and bulletin boards competed with sofas and coffee tables for space. A graduate student, thin and pale, emerged from the study to make a series of swoops and arrows with a marker on one of the glyph posters.

At dinner, Yanina suggested her husband tell their visitors about his work.

"Ah. Yes," said the linguist.

"My colleagues," the scowling scholar waved in the general direction of the study "and I are attempting to remove the veil of mathematics from the Copan narrative.

"The High Maya empire ended abruptly in the Ninth century. No one knows why.

"Fascinating," said Sasha with the Red Hair.

"Yes. It is," acknowledged Knorozov.

"As the city was falling, a scribe named Bird Jaguar was able to hide the codex – the key to the of the tablets, on which their histories were written.

"The codex has just been unearthed.

"Hence all the excitement.

"We have just today received copies of the stelae. The glyphs, you see.

"It was buried during a great battle by a scribe whom we call Bird Jaguar. Yet it is written in some kind of code."

"Mathematical in nature," added Yanina.

"B 15 Parrot," commented Knorozov.

"A veil of numbers hangs over the syllabary," he complained. "We cannot decipher the damned Astronomics — "

"Astronomics!" exclaimed young Lev. "Why, Uly won a prize for just tha — "

A loud ringing sound filled the flat. The visitors looked around.

"You have your own telephone!" exclaimed Sasha.

Knorozov abruptly abandoned his guests to hold an urgent conversation regarding Zac Cul, the number three, Kafiristan and the unearthing of a weapon called a *bahlum*.

He did not return.

Well after midnight, Uly stood at one of the desks.

She tilted the lamp so she could see more clearly.

She wore one of her father's oversized flannel shirts.

Uly smoothed out the paper of the Maya codex reproduction.

Uly could see it now.

All was quiet.

Through the far windows were visible a row of streetlights spawning pools of white snow on the wet brown-black asphalt, in the parking lot of the Performing Arts school.

Carefully, Uly wrote three notes on small squares of paper. She attached them to specific symbols on the enlarged codex photocopy.

After some thought , she added a fourth.

A Car Ride To The Vavilov Prize

*The Soviet Union's launching of Sputnik 25 ...
on Oct. 4, 1957, sent the American education
establishment into a tailspin.*

— J. ROSENBLATT, POST-SPUTNIK EDUCATION

It was well before dawn when Uly looked out the parlor windows and saw the little Peugeot pull up.

She waved, standing in the window.

The French-made car's headlights blinked.

She had assumed that Father would join her for the award ceremony. It was a great honor, for her, for their family. But he had declined, saying he hated traffic, Party officials, the city of Moscow and all Muscovites and just wanted to go home.

She closed the door quietly behind her. She descended the flights of stairs, emerging in the night. Light snow dusted her wool hat and mittens as she trotted to the car.

She opened the Peugeot's door and climbed in.

Her escort's name was Artyem. He was in his early twenties, with a quick smile and too-long hair.

"We're going to Roskosmos," announced Artyem. "The Institute. It's about forty minutes north.

She warmed her hands on the heated air.

They traversed Yazykov Circle and headed north-northwest, past the Kurchatov, past the airport

"I liked your conversion-to-parsecs tables," said Artyem.

"That was in the seventh footnote!" said Uly. "You must have read it carefully … "

"We all did," he replied.

"How did you derive those proofs for the orbits?" asked Artyem.

"The mathematics you blocked out, to draw conclusions about regular and elliptic orbits. How did you do that?"

"I just wanted to divide out separate things," explained Uly. "The different parts of the orbit calculations. Sets of angles, sets of motion, sets of eccentricities. Put them in different buckets. Then we could arrive at a numerical way to find periodic orbits for the satellites' relative motion. Using time domain."

"And where did all this business about sets and subsets come from?"

"My Mother. She helped.

"She's a math teacher. She reads the journals."

Few cars shared the streets so early.

They crossed the Ostozhenka and slowed as they turned onto the narrow side street adjacent to the Monastery.

The famous high towers and onion domes and regal open spaces of Red Square came into view.

At the checkpoint, two guards reviewed their credentials. One of them, a female, opened the gate. She waved and smiled as they passed through.

"I wanted to take you through here on the way," bragged Artyem.

Uly sat forward in her seat, craning her neck to see everything. The falling snow lent a fairy-tale aspect to the silent scene as they moved slowly through.

"I'm trying to impress you," he explained.

"Such banter," blushed Uly. "I don't know how to talk like that."

"I grew up on a farm," she added. "In Vologda Oblast."

"We're not so different," said Artyem. "I grew up in a cabin on the Yenesey. Halfway to Mongolia.

"My grandfather brought me to Moscow after I solved a two-column proof in first grade."

The Peugeot's headlights illuminated the eastern wall of the Kremlin building.

Uly glanced at her companion.

Aryem smiled.

We two will get along just fine, his smile seemed to say.

They exited Red Square through the northeastern gate.

The little French car moved steadily through the Russian night, towards dawn.

Sputnik, two months earlier, had changed everything.

The world's first artificial satellite was launched October 4, 1957. The size of a volleyball, Sputnik only remained in orbit three weeks before its batteries ran out. Yet it served as a vivid demonstration that mankind could reach the stars.

The fact that the Soviets launched the first space satellite before any American effort was not lost upon the world. It was a point of deep pride among the Russians, who had lost 27 million in the Great War, so recent, only to see the West congratulate themselves on D-Day and Dunkirk over and over until those were the only stories, and Stalingrad was forgotten.

Within the Soviet system, Sputnik spurred an entirely new look at mathematics and how it was taught. Mathematics had opened the galaxy. Now mankind was hungry for more.

TSNIIMash, the Central Research Institute of Machines, home of the Roskosmos space initiative, looked more like a summer camp than a scientific research center.

The Central Research Institute of Machines seemed composed of one modern building surrounded by log cabins and a longhouse, or lodge.

The banquet for the Vavilov prize-winners was a warm affair, like a family reunion. Tapestries on the lodge walls represented all the Asiatic tribes. Uly met all of the scientists, as well as all of their wives and families.

Sergey Korolev, the jolly head designer of Russia's rocket program, warmly congratulated the ten high-school winners of the Vavilov, one by one. He mentioned their hometowns and told a little story about their work.

Uly came last.

"And finally, we honor Ulyana Prouskieff of the Chernozem ... for her paper, Newton and the Mathematics of Satellite Motion. A remarkable little piece of work.

"Simply put, her thesis sounds straightforward: the mass of the central body (Earth) and the radius of the orbit affect orbital speed. The orbital radius is in turn dependent upon the height of the satellite above the earth.

"But in the innovative mathematical reasoning which Uly has used to reach her proof, the Committee has found a wellspring of fresh perspective. It is the promise of a new generation. A new generation of explorers. A toast!" Sergey Korolev raised his glass.

"They say the Americans produce the best science. A tradition of liberty and risk-taking and the attitude that you can change anything, do anything. So they say.

"Well, this is the best of Russian thinking. This is the kind of fearless science the Republic will need to reach Mars. And beyond.

"Yes, thank you, Mikhail. Good. Force does in fact equal mass time acceleration. Good for you. And it only took you three drinks to come up with that?

"Ulyana, would you stand and say a few words ..."

Uly stood by her seat and thanked the Committee, and her mother. She made a joke about black holes and black earth. She said she was proud to make a contribution in such excellent company. She sat down, blushing. Artyem clapped and whistled. The room applauded warmly, for hers was a brief paper, only nine pages, and they had all read it.

Morning In A Moezey Moskvi Apartment

To say that NKVD is 'a state within the state'
is to downplay the importance of the NKVD.

— ABDURAKHMAN AVTORKHANOVP
FATHER OF THE NKVD (SOVIET SECRET POLICE)

L ife stirred slowly in the Knorozov apartment.
Ever so gradually, the sun rose. Suspended motes of dust swirled in those first rays of light.

The murmuring assistants made coffee. They returned to the study.

Thirty minutes later, Sasha and Lev made tea and toast. Sasha found some fruit jam and served it on Father's toast.

In a cloud of cigarette smoke, Knorozov emerged from the study. He strode to and fro, ignoring everyone, deep in thought.

Sasha and Lev played Durak amidst a quiet shuffling of cards.

Father read a newspaper, rare enough in the Tambov Oblast, and smoked his pipe.

Yuri Knosorov strode into the kitchen to tend the whistling teapot.

He stopped with a theatrical lurch.

There, on the dining room table lay a freshly drawn facsimile of the codex.

Four handwritten notes were neatly attached

"What is this — ?" the great linguist exclaimed.

Here is what the four notes said:

NOTE 1

This is the American Zero.

NOTE 2

Base-20.

NOTE 3

Transit of Venus

NOTE 4

$$\underset{\rule{1.2em}{1.2pt}}{5} \;+\; \underset{\underset{\rule{1.2em}{1.2pt}}{\bullet\bullet\bullet}}{8} \;=\; \underset{\overset{\rule{1.2em}{1.2pt}}{\underset{\rule{1.2em}{1.2pt}}{}}}{\underset{\bullet\bullet\bullet}{13}}$$

"WHO DID THIS?" demanded Knosorov.

His associates scrambled from the den to see …

"*Transit of Venus?*" asked one of the young associates.

"Who wrote these notes? Was it one of you?"

The graduate students shook their heads ...

"Well, I did!" said Sasha.

"I hope you don't mind," she added, demurely.

"I couldn't sleep."

"Mind!" exclaimed the great linguist. "Why, this is – a— "

"A breakthrough," cried one of the young scholars. .

"Why, it's revolutionary !!" declared Knorozov. "With this, we can topple the typical-thinking Bolshevik trolls — "

He stared at the glyphs anew.

"Phonetic decipherment!! Now it's so close I can feel it !"

"The wheels are turning," said one of the pale young men. "I can see the Base 20 sequences emerge — "

"Now that we know to look for them ..." added another.

"If we can remove the veil of math," declared Knorozov. "Anything is possible!"

"Let the goose-stepping IDIOTS search, blind-folded. In the dark," Knorozov continued. "We will HIDE this from them.

"You were here!" the great linguist congratulated his assistants. "You were with me when I — "

Wham!

Without warning the front door slammed open —

Not so much 'open' but rather smashed in, hinges splintered.

The broken-apart door pieces toppled and fell into the parlor along with a rush of shouting men in dark suits —

The clamor and chaotic noise spread though the apartment space.

"What! Is! The meaning of this?" demanded Yuri Knorozov in protest. "Who do you th — "

"You're under arrest," barked the leader, a burly agent with shiny black shoes. A Tokarev TT-33 pistol was in his lead hand — no fancy artifact, this was a rugged, combat weapon, made not for show but for everyday use.

A second grouping of dark-suited intruders loudly emerged from the laundry room

An intruder barked a running report on the raid into a bulky two-way radio —

Metal cuffs snapped onto Knorozov's wrists —

The lead agent spat a term sounding like Inakomy vashiv that meant something like 'dissident' but much worse.

Sasha was yanked from her seat.

"You, too, Math Girl — "

Cards went flying. Little Lev rushed to defend his sister and was shoved away.

One of the heavy window-curtains toppled.

Father lunged and tried to wrestle his daughter away and got a broken nose for his efforts.

"Please! Please! *Comrades* — " wailed Yanina in protest. One of the intrudes scoffed at the term. Right word, wrong usage ...

Knorozov himself had gone pale and silent. Two agents had picked him up bodily so they could carry him away quickly.

The graduate students sputtered and called out, trying to form a coherent argument, but no charges had been made, and the men of the NKVD have no knack for conversation.

As for Sasha, it was not until she saw the stricken look on Father's face as she was handcuffed and pushed through the doorway, that she began to understand the dimensions of her hubris.

The radio crackled.

Sasha with the Red Hair called out for her family.

Real fear laced her voice.

They were gone.

An Unexpected Offer

*Science and math reportedly receive more attention in
the Soviet Union than in any other country.
Math is introduced in the first grade ...*

— J. Rosenblatt, Post-Sputnik Education

"Ulyana," said Artyem.
"We have an offer for you."

They were sitting in oversized cushioned chairs in front of the fireplace in the lodge.

He handed her an envelope.

"My boss has authorized me to offer you a seat on the New Mathematics Commission.

"It's a three-year position."

She opened the letter. It was a formal offer and cited a generous salary. A seal of the Institute graced the top alongside a blue-and-gold spaceship, an old-fashioned design left over from the rocket craze of the 1920's.

"There has been much discussion of how we teach mathematics in Russia. Too much memorization. Not enough critical thinking. Not enough about what the numbers mean. What the numbers do. Our schools are tied to the old methods.

"The Minister has asked us to design a campaign, a new attitude towards mathematics. New teaching methods.

"You would be an ideal member of the team. Young. Accomplished. A fresh face.

"You belong here. This is your family."

"Where would I live?" asked Uly.

"Any one of the cottages on our grounds. You family could join you.

"Yes," Uly replied. "My mother. My brother, Lev."

"Is there anyone else?"

She looked out at the night

"No," said Ulyana.

Far above, parsecs above the wood-shingled roof of the lodge, Venus shifted in her orbit, no more than a single standard deviation, then returned to her proper trajectory.

"Just those two."

Epilogue: Mayans Bury A Tablet

And nobody knows
Tiddely-Pom
How cold my toes
Tiddely-Pom
How cold my toes are growing.

— A.A. MILNE

From her hiding place, Bird Jaguar squinted at the giant, jagged-toothed barbarian.

Tillers' blood dripped crimson from his sword and shield. The barbarian grunted. He looked around, searching the battlefield for Bird Jaguar and her sister and protector, Zac Cul.

"Come, little Toads!" bellowed the barbarian. "Let the Dark Gods embrace us together!"

The prophecies did not mention him, noted Bird Jaguar to herself.

She looked up. Far overhead, a flock of blackbirds split apart and rejoined.

In this year of 8. 17. 14. 12. 11, the Fifth Lord had risen from his slumbers.

The ruination of the High Maya had begun.

"Why is he even following us?" Bird Jaguar asked Zac Cul, her older sister.

Copper bands adorned their upper arms. They were free-women, tillers, valued members of a farming clan.

"I don't know," answered Zac Cul. She dried the hilt of her sword in her skirt. "Something about us must irritate him."

This bloodthirsty, too-tall, too-strong warrior had for some reason tracked the two sisters all the way from the burning City, far from his barbarian cohort. He seemed intent on their deaths.

"You are often irritating," said Bird Jaguar to her sister.

The Emperor had murdered his own advisors, who foretold dangers that could not be seen, or proven, and then been killed by those same dangers. The throne had fallen. The City was descending into lunacy. It had all been predicted, in the stars (with certain errors), in the detailed celestial charts. The movement of Venus across the night skies had been insightful.

The prophecies did not mention him, noted Bird Jaguar to herself.

The Tillers would find a new home, new soils for their rows of vegetables and grains, in the northern hills. All would proceed, according to the fates. Most of Bird Jaguar's tribe were already on their way north.

All that was left now was to bury the codex.

The two girls were trapped in a rocky maze of ravines and caves. Bird Jaguar, a valued scribe, held fast to the codex tablet. It must be hidden, and well-hidden, for future readers.

Since birth, Zac Cul had been the younger girl's escort and protector.

This cave would do. But this entrance was unprotected.

The giant would see them —

"I thought you said you were telling our story," said Zac Cul, as she glanced over the tablet and its complex pattern of glyphs.

"These are just numbers."

"Our story is hidden behind a scrim of numbers," replied Bird Jaguar.

"Really?"

Bird Jaguar nodded.

"Am I in it?" asked Zac Cul.

"Yes. You are prominent, sister."

Losing her patience. Zac Cul shouted and rushed out of their hiding place to engage the giant —

The barbarian's eyes widened when he saw her approach —

He charged, with his bahlum hatchet raised to strike –

Seemingly out of nowhere, a soldier came hurtling down the rockface from above, landing with a thud and sweeping the barbarian's legs out from under him.

Nimbly, the soldier rose, quicker than the clumsy giant. He stabbed the barbarian through the throat before the big man could get his balance.

The giant roared in pain. Choking, he writhed and swung his limbs violently to and fro ...

But the soldier would not relent.

"You shouldn't have followed my girls," the soldier, Smoking-Frog, told his dying enemy. "You should have stayed with your friends ... "

Smoking-Frog was the girls' grandfather.

The barbarian died there, gurgling, reaching out, far from his home. A grisly death.

"Let's go," urged Smoking-Frog. "Let's bury this tablet and get out. Blackbirds are on the move." Grandfather thought it wise to coordinate

with the creatures whenever possible. They know things we don't, he would say.

Inside the cave, Bird Jaguar filled in the hollow where she had hidden the codex.

Our descendants will find this... but not for many cycles.

Bird Jaguar smiled to herself.

They will need to be clever, if they want to read it ...

Zac Cul called.

"Coming!" said Bird Jaguar.

Akbal
Cumhu
Kan

TOM'S NOTES

This is a sort of trap-door story, the true floor being the Maya flashback.

This story actually features two girl mathematicians, the Maya girl (Bird Jaguar) in the Epilogue as well as Tatiana, in Moscow 1957. Both ends of the story are about family, the loyalties and betrayals of family.

Like many oligarchies, Soviet Russia was marked by neighbors spying on neighbors. The agency represented here, NKVD, was a precursor to the more infamous KGB – both government agencies whose mission was to suppress all dissent. To silence all critics. Intellectuals like Knosorov would be tagged for surveillance. The woman on the train might have hoped for a commendation, or extra portions of groceries, for betraying Tatiana's family. The scientists of the space program would be protected from such spying because of their work on Sputnik.

The real Tatiana Proskoriakoff was sometimes called "The Accidental Mayanist." Proskouriakoff made her greatest contribution by going against the current and discovering the true literary and historical nature of Maya hieroglyphic writing. Once the codex was solved, its code broken, we found that the Maya had constructed a colossal system of mathematics and astronomy, dividing time in calendars and precise katuns, or cycles.

The situation was further complicated by Knorozov's paper appearing during the height of the Cold War, and many were able to dismiss his paper as being founded on misguided Marxist-Leninist ideology and polemic. Indeed, in keeping with the mandatory practices of the time

I don't understand the Maya-Russian connection, but it seems to be a flourishing one.

In addition to Knosorov and Proskouriakoff, Maya scholars like American Linda Schele and Englishman Eric Thompson contributed to the breaking-the-code effort, along with many others. The collective journey has been called "one of the great stories of twentieth century scientific discovery."

My little band of Maya tillers fleeing the doomed city reappears in the Botany stories.

The End

MATH
π
GIRLS

BIOS

Tom Durwood is a teacher, writer and editor with an interest in history. Tom most recently taught English Composition and Empire and Literature at Valley Forge Military College, where he won the *Teacher of the Year* Award five times. Tom has taught Public Speaking and Basic Communications as guest lecturer for the Naval Special Warfare Development Group at the Dam's Neck Annex of the Naval War College.

Tom's ebook *Empire and Literature* matches global works of film and fiction to specific quadrants of empire, finding surprising parallels. Literature, film, art and architecture are viewed against the rise and fall of empire. In a foreword to *Empire and Literature*, postcolonial scholar Dipesh Chakrabarty of the University of Chicago calls it "imaginative and innovative." Prof. Chakrabarty writes that "Durwood has given us a thought-provoking introduction to the humanities." His subsequent book "Kid Lit: An Introduction to Literary Criticism" has been well-reviewed. "My favorite nonfiction book of the year," writes The Literary Apothecary (Goodreads).

Early reader response to Tom's historical fiction adventures has been promising. "A true pleasure ... the richness of the layers of Tom's novel is compelling," writes Fatima Sharrafedine in her foreword to "The Illustrated Boatman's Daughter." The Midwest Book Review calls that same adventure "uniformly gripping and educational ... pairing action and adventure with social issues." Adds Prairie Review, "A deeply intriguing, ambitious historical fiction series."

Tom briefly ran his own children's book imprint, Calico Books (Contemporary Books, Chicago). Tom's newspaper column "Shelter" appeared in the *North County Times* for seven years. Tom earned a Masters in English Literature in San Diego, where he also served as Executive Director of San Diego Habitat for Humanity.

Two of Tom's books, "Kid Lit" and "The Illustrated Boatman's Daughter," were selected "Best of the New" by Julie Sara Porter's *Bookworm Book* Alert 2021.

https://juliesaraporterbookworm.blogspot.com/2022/01/best-of-best-new-book-alert-2021.html?m=1

Bonus: Tom interview: https://www.circumlocution.net/2021/08/interview-with-thomas-durwood.html

Sandra Uve, author of "Superwomen, Superinventors: Brilliant Ideas that Transformed our Lives" has agreed to write a 400-word Foreword to *The Math Girls*.

An exhibit based on Sandra's book about female inventors from history has been shown at more than 200 libraries and museums such as Caixaforum Zaragoza, Palma, Girona, Tarragona and Lleida. The Commonwealth of Pamplona hosted "Discovering Women Scientists" in 2021, and that same year, the *Gerència de Serveis de Biblioteques de la Diputació de Barcelona* produced an exhibition by Sandra, *Dones de la Mar*, about marine biologists and environmental activists.

Mai Nguyen is a rising illustrator of innovative work in concept art, animation and illustration. Mai studied in Singapore, where she discovered many types of art and animation. She now lives and works in Ho Chi Minh City. "The city is bursting with life and always vibrant. The chaos of a developing country means more opportunities, more corners to discover."

Mai's work also appears in Tom's ambitious trilogy set in the American Revolution, "The Illustrated Colonials."

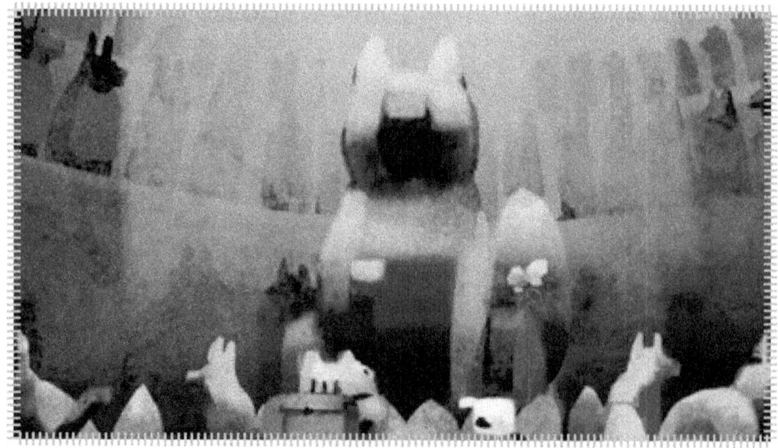

An example of Mai's animation work.

The Science Girls
The Aviation Girls

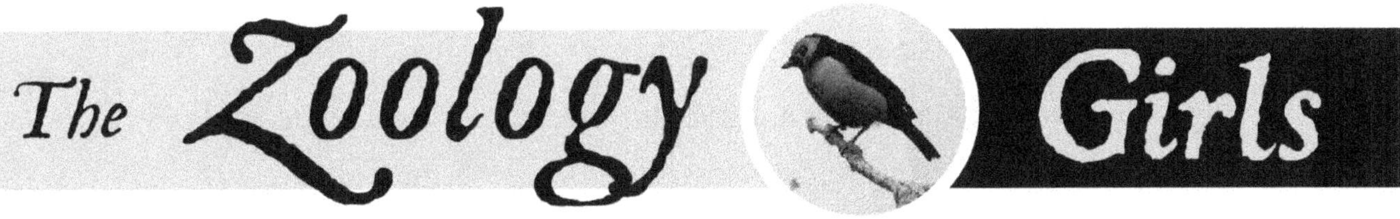
The Zoology Girls
The Botany Girls

Readers' comments on Tom's historical fiction

Exceedingly polished and well-crafted story. Meticulously researched ... complex and interesting.

-- Sarah Park Rankin, Common Threads

Luminous ... the story is encompassing, intelligent and layered.

-- Pharoah Miles, Graphic Policy Reviews

A work of great scope and adventure. The reach is far ...
An engaging series . . . We see the ripple effects of history.

-- Christopher Hoitash, author of "A Sister's Habit"

Wow ... unexpected. Skillful and entertaining.

-- Zara Miller, author of " I Am Cecilia"

The Colonials is clearly well-researched, containing the high-octane adventure quotient of a James Michener novel and the imaginative complexity of a Harry Potter tale.

-- Marta Chang, Independent Book Reviews

Gorgeously written ... the author has done his research. The characters are clever, self-driven, and unique. These books are sure to spark curious minds.

-- Kerri Irish, ComfyReader book blog

Compelling ... surprising ... strong characterization ... a powerful draw.
Absorbing ... young readers of historical fiction will relish.

-- Diane Donovan, Midwest Book Review

Very literary, almost poetic writing and near flawless editing. I can see this book having wide-ranging appeal, not just teens, but also for adults as well. Highly recommended.

-- Claire Middleton (Goodreads; Barnes & Noble; Indie Book Reviewers)

Tom Durwood is the real thing.

-- Joe Weber, Honorable Enemies, Rules of Engagement

The debut of a wonderful writer ...

-- Laraine Herring, Monsoons, Lost Fathers, and Lay My Sorrow Down

A deeply intriguing, ambitious historical fiction series.

-- Prairie Review

STEM-BASED HISTORICAL FICTION

THE ADVENTURES OF
RUBY PI
AND THE
GEOMETRY
GIRLS

BY TOM DURWOOD

Teen Heroines in History Use Geometry, Algebra and Other Mathematics to Solve Colossal Problems
FOREWORD BY SANDRA UVE

The Adventures of Ruby Pi and the Geometry Girls

A robust entry into the YA field, this first "Ruby Pi" collection of adventures tells of brave heroines fighting tremendous odds, using the one tool that can save them – mathematics.

From ancient India to World War II, from Sputnik-era Moscow to the Benin Kingdoms and the Jim Crow South, clever girls overcome huge odds to save their families.

Few works of fiction truly transport the reader to another place and time, and even fewer give that reader something they can take back home afterwards. 'Geometry Girls' achieves both, breaking down barriers in educational literature and making mathematics not only interesting, but a matter of life and death. **Tom has done his homework ... this work will be a treasure of school libraries everywhere in years to come.**

Written with a skillful hand and with the kind of attention to detail that will grip an ambitious teenager.

The MLK story ... an excellent story with a crucially important message for young people in modern Western society. **The mathematics is simple but elegant.**

-- Graham Van Goffrier, third-year PhD candidate (Theoretical neutrino physics)

www.themathgirls.com

THE ADVENTURES OF
RUBY PI
AND THE
MATH GIRLS

BY TOM DURWOOD

Teen Heroines in History Use Geometry, Algebra and Other Mathematics to Solve Colossal Problems

FOREWORD BY SANDRA UVE

The Adventures of Ruby Pi and the Math Girls

The second volume in this twin work, "The Adventures of Ruby Pi and the Math Girls" delivers five ambitious, not-for-everyone adventures to take young readers deep into mathematics and history. Our critical-thinking heroines are thrust into vivid settings from Mao's retreat to the cowboy West, from London to Palenque. Can they math their way out?

In this outstanding collection, Tom addresses the chronic problem of our young women dropping out of STEM studies. His stories lend adventure to scientific thinking.

"Sasha with the Red Hair" is thoughtful and surprising, like all Tom' s stories.

Exceptional ... a family drama disguised as an adventure.

-- Tanzeela Siddique, Math Teacher

www.themathgirls.com

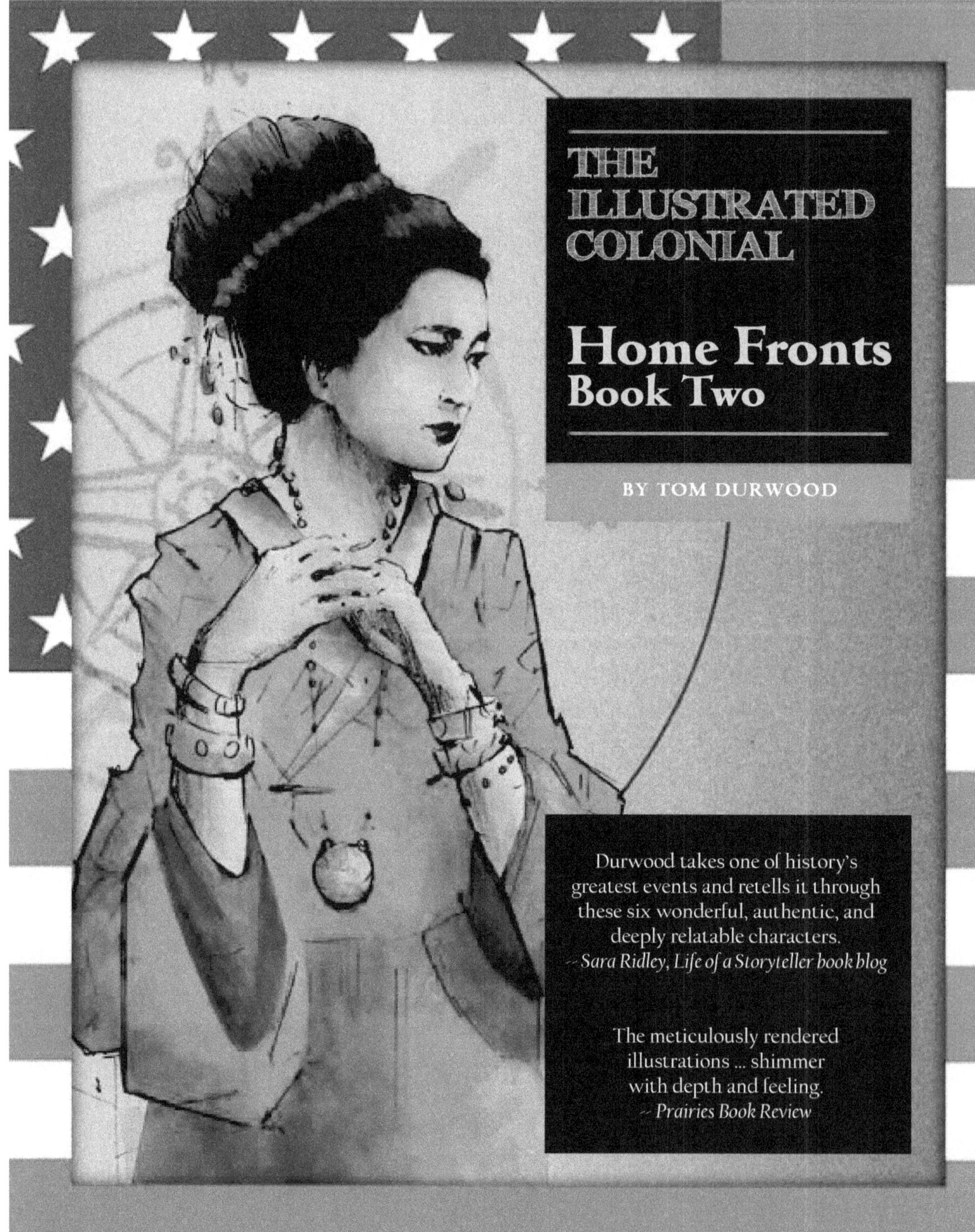
THE ILLUSTRATED COLONIAL
Home Fronts
Book Two
BY TOM DURWOOD
Durwood takes one of history's
greatest events and retells it through
these six wonderful, authentic, and
deeply relatable characters.
~Sara Ridley, Life of a Storyteller book blog
The meticulously rendered
illustrations ... shimmer
with depth and feeling.
~Prairies Book Review

The Illustrated Colonials Trilogy

A new perspective one on of history's most fascinating moments. This richly illustrated trilogy captures some of the global thrill and tumult caused by the American Revolution. The epic tale follows six young rich kids from around the world as they join the cause, finding love and treachery along the path. Unique entry into the robust YA universe.

A deeply intriguing, ambitious historical fiction series.

-- Prairie Review

Clever .... Durwood's deeply realized characters are sketched with precision and care.

- Books Coffee Reviews

www.mycolonials.com

The Illustrated Boatman's Daughter

An Egyptian girl fights intrigue and corruption for the completion of the world's greatest man-made waterway. Illustrated edition of a young-adult novella with 40 original color pieces. An attention-getting story featuring multicultural characters and settings. Classic adventure starring a smart, strong heroine.

"A true pleasure. The richness of the layers of Tom's novel is compelling."

-- Fatima Sharrafedine, in her Foreword

"Uniformly gripping and educational ... pairing action and adventure with social issues."

--The Midwest Book Review

www.boatmansdaughter.com

ULYSSES S. GRANT IN CHINA
1879
THE ILLUSTRATED ULYSSES S. GRANT IN CHINA & other stories
BY TOM DURWOOD
ILLUSTRATED BY
Boell Oyino
Well-Bee
Sigurd Fernstrom

The Illustrated 'Ulysses S. Grant in China' and Other Stories

Heroes coming of age... and changing history.

A lushly illustrated collection of stories from turning points in history, the adventures of brave teen protagonists trying desperately to meet the moment.

Poison and pistols, thieves and treachery, bandits and naval battles, opium dens and mysterious Caliphs and love triangles — readers will find it all in this colorful collection.

"All the makings of a wonderful literary property."

-- Sherri Smith, Park Road Books

www.usginchina.com

WITH A CURSE, I SHOULDERED MY WAY THROUGH A STOUT DOORWAY ON OUR RIGHT.

King James' Seventh Company

Yes, the obstacles are many, and time is short for the six young members of King James' Seventh Company. To save Six Companies of scholars, this fellowship of teenagers must cross a most dangerous landscape.

It begins as the simplest of stories: a young book-keeper (Matthias) is loaned out to one of his firm's clients. It seems there is some confusion in the client's ledgers. Matthias soon finds that the client is the King of England, and there is far more amiss in his kingdom than the ledgers. Dark and deadly forces swirl within Westminster Abbey, where the eminent scholars of the day are assembled to produce the world's greatest book: The King James Bible.

The novel's story-within-a-story is a sweeping account of Paul's real life, painting a very different portrait of the man who so effectively spread his version of Christianity.

Very literary, almost poetic writing and near flawless editing ... the author's narrative prose was some of the best and most authentic I've read in a while. (5 stars)

-- Claire Middleton, Goodreads; Barnes & Noble; Indie Book Reviewers

USEFUL FOR ANYONE INTERESTED IN LITERATURE. COMPLEX IDEAS ARE PRESENTED CLEARLY.
AMAZING …
SHARING THE WONDERS OF LITERATURE AND THE TOOLS FOR UNPACKING HOW LITERATURE WORKS … AN AESTHETIC JOURNEY.
THIS IS LITERARY CRITICISM AT ITS LEAST FORMAL AND MOST LIVELY. IT WILL DEFINITELY CHALLENGE YOU AND YOUR STUDENTS.
"KID LIT" IS AN AUTHENTIC LOVE OF LITERATURE
WHAT COMES THROUGH THE PAGES OF "KID LIT" IS AN AUTHENTIC LOVE OF LITERATURE READERS AND TEACHERS ALIKE WILL FIND IN IT A USEFUL AND WORTHWHILE RESOURCE.
GET READY TO DIVE IN AND ENJOY A NEW PERSPECTIVE TO LITERATURE.
KID LIT IS AN ABSOLUTELY VALUABLE SCHOLARLY RESOURCE.
DURWOOD'S WORK IS USEFUL FOR BOTH STUDENT AND TEACHER,
Kid Lit
AN INTRODUCTION TO LITERARY CRITICISM
— ADVANCE REVIEW COPY — NOT FOR SALE
TOM DURWOOD
TEACHERS AT THE MIDDLE SCHOOL AND HIGH SCHOOL LEVEL HAVE A POWERFUL TOOL AT THEIR DISPOSAL.
THIS WAS MY FAVORITE NONFICTION BOOK OF THE YEAR BY FAR
THERE IS A REFRESHING PLAINESS AND ACCESSIBILITY THAT TODAY'S BEST TEACHING AND ACADEMIC PROSE ARE MADE OF.
THERE IS A HANDMADE QUALITY TO DURWOOD'S TWO NEW BOOKS …
"KID LIT" NAVIGATES A BROAD BODY OF WORK TO INTRIGUING EFFECT. I FOUND IMPRESSIVE HIS FAMILIARITY WITH WORKS OF THE PAST FOUR CENTURIES AND HIS ABILITY TO PUT THEM IN INTRIGUING DIALOG. HE IS JUST AS COMFORTABLE WITH THE BROTHERS GRIMM AS HE IS WITH THE HUNGER GAMES, AND THOUGHTFULLY LISTS BOOKS AND FILMS FOR INSTRUCTORS TO TEACH AND EXPLORE.
RAISES FRUITFUL QUESTIONS ABOUT CHILDREN'S LITERATURE, FILM AND CONTEMPORARY MEDIA …
WHAT COMES THROUGH "KID LIT" IS AN AUTHENTIC LOVE OF LITERATURE THE PAGES OF "KID LIT" IS AN AUTHENTIC LOVE OF LITERATURE. READERS WILL FIND IN IT LITERATURE ALIKE WILL FIND IN IT WORTHWHILE TEACHERS AND RESOURCE. A USEFUL

Kid Lit: An Introduction to Literary Theory

There are twin premises to Tom Durwood's "Kid Lit: An Introduction to Literary Criticism." The first is that literary theory is for all of us, and the second is that students can develop marketable lifetime skills when building critical thinking regarding their favorite stories.

Tom is a teacher and it is quickly evident in the clarity of his writing. He poses a simple question – for example, *What makes a good villain? --* and then draws you into a comparison between Captain Ahab (apocalyptic evil) and Dr. Octopus (simple greed). This then flows into a consideration of evil in all literature. You are then invited to formulate your own theory of good and bad by following his clear illustrations.

This is literary criticism at its least formal and most lively .... It will definitely challenge you and your students.

-- Todd Whitaker, author of "What Great Teachers Do Differently"

My favorite non-fiction book of the year, by far.

-- The Literary Apothecary

www.kidlitcrit.com

A STUDENT-FRIENDLY LENS
ON HUMANITIES

Empire and Literature

An Introduction

Tom Durwood

FOREWORD BY DIPESH CHAKRABARTY

Empire and Literature

Tom Durwood's supplemental-text e-book *Empire and Literature* promises to be an invaluable tool not only for students following his courses, but also for anyone interested to explore the deep relations between literature and empire.

Durwood brilliantly argues that literature and the workings of empire are deeply connected.

An exceptional pedagogical tool, clear and concise exposition.
-- Andrei Ionescu, PhD in Languages/Literature and Psychology, University of Padua

Durwood has indeed given us a thought-provoking introduction to the humanities. Teachers will find much here that is imaginative and innovative. I hope his book will receive the attention it deserves.
-- Dipesh Chakrabarty, The University of Chicago, from his Foreword

www.empirestudies.com

A CASE STUDY IN NARRATIVE AND EMPIRE
TEDDY'S TANTRUM
JOHN D. WEAVER AND THE EXONERATION OF THE 25TH INFANTRY
TOM DURWOOD

Teddy's Tantrum

A Case Study in Empire and Literature

This new account revisits a little-known 1906 incident in Teddy Roosevelt's administration and finds an epic "lost" story of intrigue, combat, politics and redemption.

On November 5, 1906, Roosevelt dismissed 167 members of the 25th Infantry in what historian Lewis Gould calls "one of the most glaring miscarriages of justice in American history."

Sixty years later, a journeyman writer named John D. Weaver, the son of a clerk at the 1906 hearings, embarked on a campaign to exonerate the soldiers. His book produced a small measure of justice: in February of 1973, the U.S. Army issued an apology to the men of the 25th Infantry and awarded the sole surviving battalion member (Dorsie Willis) back pay.

This is the first chronicle of the entire Brownsville story, treating Weaver and the troops' exoneration as an equal part of the narrative. Author Tom Durwood scratches the surface of "Teddy's tantrum" and finds a confluence of rich characters and enduring themes. It is a story of military heroism and redemption, loyalty and betrayal, presidential influence and the power of narrative. *Teddy's Tantrum* seeks to set the neglected episode in its historical context.

'Teddy's Tantrum' takes a period of history and shines new light on it ... Tom pulls out the grander themes of the tragedy and triumph. The true stuff of history.

-- Tim Pritchard, author "Ambush Alley"

www.teddystantrum.com

Ruby Pi and the Botany Girls

Smart and resourceful girls coming of age star in unexpected scenarios from our rich history with the plant world

This time, Ruby and her fellow heroines take on the plant kingdom and emerge with out-of-ordinary adventures and science-based resolutions. First, Ruby is drawn into an international drama while engineering a new wing of Kew Gardens. Tea plantations and poppy-field rivalries mix with the India independence movement to create a witches' brew for Rupa and her family.

In other times and places, we meet teen seed-hunters in Tibet; a young novitiate helping Gregor Mendel make sense of his experiments in genetics; a young police detective in Mexico City and his botanist sister as they fight powerful forces in a deadly intrigue over Norman Borlaug's Green Revolution on the plains of Queretaro. The Irish potato famine threatens young Marcy and her extended clan. The sudden failure of a corn crop triggers the fall of Palenque. The 'Botany Girls' collection ends with a science fiction drama regarding the future of botany.

www.themathgirls.com